Fat Girl
Dances
with Rocks

SUSAN STINSON

Also by Susan Stinson

Belly Songs: In Celebration of Fat Women

Fat Girl
Dances
with Rocks

SUSAN STINSON

spinsters ink
minneapolis

GUERNEVILLE

Spinsters Ink
P.O. Box 300170
Minneapolis, MN 55403-5170

Cover art entitled "Prana" by Jody Kim copyright © 1994
Cover design by Tara Christopherson, Fruitful Results

Production: Sacha Bush   Carolyn Law
              Melanie Cockrell   Lori Loughney
              Lynette D'Amico   Rhonda Lundquist
              Joan Drury   Stefanie Shiffler
              Kay Hong   Liz Tufte
              Kelly Kager

Pages 136–142 first appeared in a slightly different form as "Sabotage," in *Sinister Wisdom #48, Lesbian Resistance,* December 1992. The last seven lines of Chapter Nine, pages 92–93, first appeared as a poem, "Chalcedony," in *Fractals In the Arts,* Winter 1992.

Library of Congress Cataloging-in-Publication Data
Stinson, Susan
    Fat girl dances with rocks / Susan Stinson.
        p.   cm.
    ISBN 1-883523-02-8 : $10.95
    I. Title.
PS3569.T535F38   1994
813'.54—dc20   94-16522
                                                                      CIP

Printed on recycled paper.

Praise for
Fat Girl Dances with Rocks

"In this sensual, gently stinging first novel, Susan Stinson tells the story of a young fat lesbian's sweet-sharp summer of awakening to herself as an animal and moral being. Stinson's language dreams, drives, and dances, loving the taste of everything it describes—a lover's mind, an icy mountain stream, potatoes with sour cream and butter—in a thoroughly American universe. Char is a character I won't forget, who fills my heart as she begins to take in the immense truth of her own."
—Joan Larkin, author of *A Long Sound*

"Susan Stinson describes the pain and confusion of growing up fat and female in America with such compassion and honesty that I found myself sighing and nodding with recognition."
—Irene Zahava, editor of *Lesbian Love Stories* and *Word of Mouth*

Hooray for *Fat Girl Dances with Rocks!* Susan Stinson's first novel is full of big, beautiful language and not only that, her main character, Char, is one of the best teenaged heroines I've ever met. Fat, dykey, and determined, Char spends her days learning geology and her nights learning to dance. When her best pal, Felice, goes to New Mexico for the summer, Char stays behind and works full time at a nursing home. What she learns that summer about commitment, community, and honest emotion spins her on toward adulthood with magic and grace. Susan Stinson's writing is music to my ears, and *Fat Girl Dances with Rocks* makes me want to do the twist!
—Judith Katz, author of *Running Fiercely Toward A High Thin Sound*

Acknowledgments

This book would not have been possible without the energy, insights and support of members of Fly-By-Night, Valley Lesbian Writers Group, and other readers:

Janet Aalfs, Athena Andreadis, Sally Bellerose, Toni Brown, Carrie Dearborn, Susan Eschbach, Ellen Frye, Vicky Greenbaum, Chaia Zblocki Heller, Tryna Hope, Christine Ianieri, Elaine Keach, Terry McMillan, Emma Morgan, Marcie Pleasants, Amanda Powell, Patricia Roth Schwartz, Stephanie Smith, Judith Stein, Sarah Van Arsdale, Irene Zahava, and others.

I thank the Mt. Holyoke Writers Conference, and the lesbian communities in Colorado and Massachusetts that have given me so much. I thank fat activists everywhere. I thank the staff at Spinsters: Kelly Kager, Joan Drury, Lynette D'Amico, Liz Tufte, and Melanie Cockrell. I thank my family: Mollie and Bill Stinson; Donald and Barbara Stinson; Karen Stinson; Michael and Eva Stinson.

There are more reasons for tenderness and respect within these lists than I could begin to express.

For Jacqueline Yvette Morales-Ferrand

Chapter

One

FELICE LIFTED THE NEEDLE BACK TO THE start of "Last Dance," then grabbed my hand and put it on her hip. She swung her rear end back and forth to give me the beat. Her disco purse bounced against my knuckles. I whirled out when she pushed my shoulder, and tried to whirl in again without letting my breasts rub against her tank top.

She closed her eyes in concentration. "Listen to the bass," she whispered. "Here comes the hard part."

All I had to do was follow.

We had a couple of hours before Felice's parents would get home from work. She pushed me through the moves again and again: twist, step, twirl out, twirl back. We circled each other, crossing and uncrossing our arms, then bumped hips. I wanted to be in perfect time, but the whole dance moved us out of time. We had no relation to five o'clock, when we'd have to open the sliding glass door to clear out the smell of pot, when Felice would finally let the needle slide on over to the next song, when she'd have to turn on the stove and start browning the meat for her family's supper. That was never going to happen. She would keep her hand firm against my back. I would learn to understand the beat.

WHEN I GOT home, Mom was in the kitchen, stirring eggs and oatmeal into ground meat, wearing her apron with the bluebird on it that stretched across her stomach. I tucked my shirt in and popped a peppermint Lifesaver into my mouth so she wouldn't smell pot on my breath, then grabbed a handful of spoons and forks and knives. Felice and I had plans to go out after supper.

I slapped the silverware onto the table: Jeff, Dad, Mom, me. The dog always sat under the table at Mom's feet. The plates felt good—thick and dependable—but I forgot to fold the paper napkins in half. Mom gave me a look.

We edged through the meal: meatloaf and scalloped potatoes, seconds for Jeff and Dad, green beans, salad, diet dressing, and a Jell-O dessert. I left the beans on my plate, and sopped up the extra catsup with a piece of bread. I was still high enough to feel private doing this, but the eyes of the table were upon me.

"Charlotte." Mom leaned toward me across the salad bowl. "Where are your manners?"

Jeff patted his mouth with his napkin like a shocked gentleman. "She doesn't have any."

"No one asked you, Jeff." Mom sighed loudly.

Dad looked over the top of his newspaper. "Keep your mouths shut, all of you. Betty, aren't you teaching the girl anything?"

I think I actually hissed, because Jeff ostentatiously wiped spit out of his eye. I apologized, "Excuse me. I'm sorry. I should have used a spoon. Forgive me."

"That's enough," Dad told me.

Jeff wasn't finished. "Remember the time she put catsup on her angel food cake?"

"Enough." Mom's lip was quivering, so Jeff knew he had to stop. "Char," she said, "eat your beans."

AFTER CHANGING MY shirt and combing my hair, I drove the Pinto over to Felice's house. She answered the door in her bathrobe.

"I've got to take a shower," she said. "You can go watch TV with my dad, if you want." She walked down the hall into the bathroom and shut the door.

I stuck my head into the TV room. Mr. Ventura gave a hunched-up nod. "Hello, Char," he said.

"Hi, Mr. Ventura." He sank a little further into his easy chair. I felt large and hearty.

Mr. Ventura picked up the TV remote control and started switching channels. I looked down the hall toward the bathroom. The door was still shut, of course. She'd be another half hour at least. I wondered if Mr. Ventura would think I was rude if I went to wait in her room.

He was shunting back and forth between news broadcasts. "How's school?" he asked. The screen flashed three versions of the weather report in quick succession. He paused on a weatherman wearing a tie that said "COLORADO" down his chest.

"School's okay." I was getting a little dizzy, watching the TV. He looked exhausted, but kept punching buttons. I decided that he would be relieved if I moved on. "Well, see you later," I said. He winced and smiled at the same time, then gave his nod.

As I headed for Felice's room, I caught sight of Mrs. Ventura in her bedroom at the end of the hall. She was reading a magazine, flipping the pages very quickly. Her hair shone under the sharp light from her bedside lamp.

Suddenly she stopped and stared at something in the magazine. I jumped a little when she ripped the page out. She beckoned to me with her hand without looking up.

I was surprised that she had known I was standing there, but I went to her. "Hi, Mrs. Ventura." I wished Felice would hurry up.

She looked at me then, with eyes shaped exactly like Felice's. Before I knew what was happening, she stood up, grabbed my shoulders, and pushed me in front of her big mirror. She spread the magazine page across the fattest part of my stomach and held it there.

I looked into the mirror and saw that it was a picture of a model, just her shoulders and head. She had a big perm and looked very odd with Mrs. Ventura's red fingernails pressing her between the elastic waistband of my slacks and the fold where my breasts began. I looked back at Mrs. Ventura's eyes in the mirror.

"There, Char," she said. "You should get your hair done just like that."

Felice threw open the bathroom door and called my name. "Come keep me company, Char."

"Excuse me," I said to Mrs. Ventura. I went into the bathroom, feeling shaky. Steam enveloped me. Felice shut the door behind me. She had on jeans and a green shirt with silver threads, but her hair was still wet.

"I stood on the scale before I got in the shower," she said. "I've lost $2\frac{1}{2}$ pounds since yesterday."

"Great," I said, "you look great." We were on a diet together, but we had a date to cheat that night. I had lost fifteen pounds since we started, but that hadn't even begun to give me a waist.

She turned on her blow dryer. She worked her comb and hummed. The dryer made a white noise like water dropping over rocks in a long fall. It was kind of relaxing.

Felice was pulling her hair into a bun. "Have you finished *Fear of Flying* yet?" She had given me a paperback copy with all the dirty parts underlined.

"Yeah. It was hot." I raised my voice over the noise.

Felice smoothed the last tendrils behind her ears. "Much better than *The Happy Hooker*, don't you think?"

I noticed that the bones in her wrists were beginning to stand out. "Definitely. Much more class."

She shut off the dryer. I heard the voices of "Dallas" from the TV room. "Where do you want to go tonight?"

"I don't know. Somewhere fun."

Mrs. Ventura yelled behind us as we left. "Be careful, girls. Be sure to keep the car doors locked."

I put the Pinto into gear and pulled out, smooth and slow. We drove past Mrs. Peterson's. She was standing in her garden in a floppy straw hat, watering in the dusk to avoid evaporation.

She waved her hose at us. "Hi, girls."

"Hi, Mrs. Peterson."

We had always admired her flowers. She favored soft, feathery varieties in purple and red. One night three years ago, Felice and I had snuck into her yard and chewed the centers off a couple of her poppies. We were fourteen then and had heard that certain flowers would get us high. We tasted the morning-glory petals, too, but all that did was give our lips a blue tinge.

"Mrs. Peterson must have a great grief in life," said Felice now, nodding again at the solitary figure in her blue housedress surrounded by the gathering dark and her extravagant blooms. But it had been her garden we picked to crawl around in, trying to get a bite of something good.

WE DIDN'T LEAVE the Pinto all night. Driving up and down Moody Boulevard, we sang "Delta Dawn." We passed the Lucky U Motel, Jack in the Box, Hurt's Chevrolet. Felice lit a joint. I steered, out of sequence with every traffic light. We passed a billboard about a career as a dental hygienist. We put the joint in the ashtray and hit the drive-through at Arby's for a jamocha shake. I had applied there for a summer job, but you had to be eighteen to run the meat machine.

We drove on, singing in a Texas accent we used a lot that spring: "Delta DAWN, what's that flower you have ON..." over and over.

It was dark, and the moving car made a breeze. Felice lit the joint again. We were on familiar streets, moving as fast as we knew how to go, trying to feel safe. We built the song up, repeating the chorus, forgetting the verses. Felice might forget, that is. I thought I knew every word. I'd correct her. "No, it's 'she walks downtown with a suitcase in her hand, lookin' for a serious dark-haired man.'" I didn't know I had some of it wrong.

The "dawn" part was loud, then soft. We made the accent sharper, less nasal, more mysterious. The joint went out, we were singing so long. I drove, not deciding where to go, just doing the long western loop up from our suburb. By the time we got downtown, our voices were fading from "Delta Dawn," so we moved into "Let Me Be There," with a high part for me and a low part for Felice.

Chapter Two

"BOOGIE-OOGIE-OOGIE" WAS PLAYING OVER the loudspeaker in the high school cafeteria. Felice took the top slice of bread off her tuna sandwich. She ate the tuna with a fork, then stuffed the bottom slice back into her plastic baggie.

"Come on, Char," she said. "All you'd be missing is home room and Health."

I toyed with my macaroni and cheese. I'd gotten the hot lunch. "Attendance is a big deal in Health. That's all they have to grade you on."

Felice sipped her Tab. "Oh, right. They're going to flunk you because you didn't hear the lecture on sprains and ice packs." She crushed the can. "Let's go."

"They give you one unexcused absence before they call your mother." I picked up my tray.

Felice opened her pack and started rummaging for her lip gloss as we walked. "Forget about your mother. If she knew half of the things you do, she'd have a cardiac arrest."

"I know." I pressed my fists to the sides of my head and screwed up my face. "And I'm racked with guilt."

The sun was shining out in the student parking lot. Rows and rows of cars were parked on the packed dirt. I watched Felice digging in her pack for her keys and remembered the first time she mattered to me.

It was afternoon recess. We were both in second grade, but we were in different classes. I was out behind the backstop, playing with the wind.

That wasn't what I usually did at recess. I usually sat against the school building and read Louisa May Alcott books. I was into Jo and Meg and sickly Beth. Pretty, golden Amy I could have done without. Mrs. Simms, the playground monitor, put a stop to my reading. She reported me to my teacher who reported me to my mother who told me to cut it out. I was shocked. Mrs. Simms's job was to break up fights and arrest Lisa Mogul for smoking, so it was awful to come to her attention. I decided to stop giving my mother goodnight hugs in protest, but at the last minute I had to go into the living room and hug her in spite of myself.

I understood, of course. I was a fat little girl with sparkles on the corners of my glasses. Nice people called me chubby; the boys said tub of lard or fatso. Grownups who wanted the best for me didn't want me sitting and reading at recess. I was supposed to be running around playing and trying to burn off calories. But dodgeball was the rage of the playground that fall, and I hated dodgeball. Alan Gerkin could hit me in the stomach fifty times in five minutes. Mrs. Simms insisted I do something besides read, standing over me and blocking the sun until I closed the book, prodding me a little with the toe of her tennis shoe if I was slow getting up. So I took to hiding

Little Women in the waistband of my stretch pants and walking all the way across the gravel field to the backstop, where I could read in peace.

That particular fall afternoon, the sun was bright. There was a sharp, warm wind that rattled the swingset and changed the distances between me and the kids clumped up inside a chalk circle playing dodgeball, as usual. I walked steadily away from them toward the backstop, but the wind carried their shouting right along with me. Then the wind shifted, and suddenly all I could hear was the clanging swingset and the roaring of the wind itself. It rustled my clothes all around me, especially my poncho, which was loose and bright.

When I got to my usual spot, I was annoyed to see a huddle of four boys bending over something near the fence that marked the end of school property. They weren't far enough away for my liking, but they seemed intent on whatever they were doing, so I decided to ignore them.

I pulled my book out of its hiding place, but the wind fluttered the pages, and I didn't really want to read. Instead, I took off my poncho and held it over my head. It streamed out behind me, and made me feel like Sister Bertrill, the Flying Nun. I ran a little ways, straight into the wind, my poncho stretched tight and pulling against my hands. Then it felt like me flying. The sky was arching low over the playground. My hair whipped into my face, and I could taste dust on my teeth. I had to stop and breathe. I had my arms raised so high that my shirt had ridden up, and part of my stomach was out in the air. I looked down and saw that the waistband of my underpants was showing, so I glanced toward the boys. They hadn't looked up. Then, so fast it made me jump, Felice Ventura appeared. She was barreling toward the backstop, chasing a red dodgeball. Her black hair was rubberbanded into two puppydog tails that stuck out from each side of her head and bobbed wildly as she ran. She was wearing a red skirt, but it had blown up and uncovered the green shorts she had on underneath. Her skinny legs were churning. I thought she looked faster than the wind.

The ball bounced toward me, and I tried to stop it, but it hit my foot and ricocheted toward the boys. It hit the back of Alan Gerkin's leg, and he turned around and yelled something rude. He tried to grab the ball, but she was right behind it. She caught it on the rebound, screeching to a halt in front of him. She stood on tiptoe trying to see around him to the center of the huddle. When she saw what they were doing, she let out a cry and pushed him out of the way.

I watched Felice stomping the ground and cussing at the boys, but I couldn't see what had set her off. She whaled into them with her rubber ball, slapping it at their calves and arms until their skin had bright red blotches all over.

I was trying to ease away from the trouble, but when I saw Alan Gerkin pick up a handful of rock and gravel to throw at Felice, I ran at him, waving my poncho over my head, screaming at the top of my lungs. Alan threw his rocks, anyway, but the wind whipped up, and they scattered without reaching Felice. The wind must have carried my voice all the way back to the playground, because Mrs. Simms came to the edge of the blacktop blowing her whistle. The boys took off running toward the school. Felice stood her ground, and Alan knocked the ball out of her hands as he passed. I was completely out of breath, and was leaning over wheezing. Felice waited until I lifted my head, then took hold of a corner of my poncho and dragged me over to show me the anthill still boiling with red ants, and the big, flattened grasshopper that the ants were swarming over.

"They pulled the grasshopper's legs off," Felice told me. "They were feeding it alive to the ants. I had to smash it."

The whistle blew again, louder, and I looked up to see Mrs. Simms starting across the field. I elbowed Felice, and she ran out to head Mrs. Simms off. I followed as fast as I could. All of us, even the boys, knew it was no good getting adults in on a life-and-death thing like this.

Felice and I were friends.

SHE FINALLY UNLOCKED the door of her mother's green Mustang and spent a long time moving books off the seat and checking her makeup in the mirror before she reached across and opened the door for me.

"Thanks," I said.

"Sorry," said Felice, two beats late.

We drove to the vast Safeway parking lot and sat in the car, psyching up.

Felice handed me a couple of dollars. "You buy the beer," she said. "You look older than me."

My hands were shaking as I took the money. I hated breaking the law. Felice and I called this my problem with authority, and I was trying to overcome it.

"Okay," I said, "but we should buy some other stuff, too. Not just beer. Beets, powdered milk. Something respectable."

Felice had taken out her raspberry lip gloss and was greasing her lips. "Don't be so paranoid. People buy beer every day."

We walked down the long, clean, well-lighted aisles of the supermarket. The aisles were full of women who moved so slow they looked like they were dancing, or else dreaming. They pulled out cartons of chocolate milk, cold white packs of green beans, red mounds of ground meat. The small children in their carts were alert as they scanned the shelves, searching for boxes they recognized. "This! Quisp!" Everyone looked familiar. I picked up a box of Velveeta.

"Not that." Felice waved a tub of sour cream at me. "Something real."

We made it through the checkout line with our sour cream and Doritos and our Scotch Buy beer. I felt exhilarated as the electric doors slid open in front of us. We had gotten away with something. I bumped Felice with my hip. She bounced off, right into the drug store.

"Shit." I was not in the mood to look at makeup. I never wore it except when I could get Felice to put it on for me. She always spent hours poring over *Cosmo* and *Vogue* and *Glamour,* so she was an expert. She had very informed fingers. If I caught her in the right mood, she would pull my hair back and slide her cool hands up my cheeks, telling me when to pucker, when to blink. She used pads and brushes that left color in small, stiff strokes. She was trying to get me to take an interest.

But she wasn't heading into Rexall now for the sake of my development. I usually had to get her drunk and wheedle for an hour before she would agree to do my face. I thought she must want a specific little beige bottle of something, so I followed her inside.

She was looking at hair dyes. "Felice! You wouldn't!" Her thick black hair wouldn't take henna. It rolled right off like water on tar.

She picked up a box and examined the picture. "Actually, I wouldn't mind being a blonde, but that's not what I came in here for. I'm just stalling. I'm going to buy a *Playgirl.*"

12

I stared at the shelf full of smiling models with variations on blonde, lustrous hair. "You are? You mean you're really going to do it?"

Felice compared honey to platinum. "Yeah. Don't you want me to?"

I watched her hold the boxes up next to her face. "Of course, yeah. I just can't believe you've really got the nerve."

She put the boxes back and jiggled the shopping bag against her hip, so I could hear the beer slosh in the cans. "We're on a roll." She laughed. The clerk looked up.

Felice had the gift of instant matter-of-factness. "Okay, now."

I took the Safeway sack. "I'll wait outside."

She grabbed one of my belt loops and towed me along behind her to the magazine rack. She picked up a copy of *Cosmo.* We knew *Playgirl* was kept under the counter. We'd noticed it before.

The clerk was putting prices on nail polish with a label gun. She was fat and wore a loose blue smock. Her hair was either "Moon Mist" or "White Sands."

Felice slapped the *Cosmo* down on the counter, the cover girl's slick nipples glaring. She used her most arrogant tone. "This and a *Playgirl.*"

The clerk reached behind her and brought a copy back without looking up. She rang up the total, then her eyes flicked at me. I wanted to smile, but that seemed like a risk.

"That's four dollars." The clerk slid the magazines into a bag and counted out the change. I wondered who weighed more, her or me.

"Thank you," said Felice, and we made our escape.

WE DROVE UP to Tuckers Park. Its reputation as a hangout drew us as much as the fact that it was full of secluded places to park. We sat in the car and read the fantasies aloud to each other. The featured penises were called "lollipops" and "joysticks." We speculated about which were circumcised and which weren't. We didn't know how to tell the difference. Felice told me her cousin Mickey had tried oral sex once and thrown up. We drank the beer and ate the sour cream and Doritos as we flipped through the magazines. We got vaguely drunk as it got dark. We each had to get home in time to eat supper with the folks, but Felice wanted to climb some rocks first. She was interested in geology. I didn't really want to leave the warm car, but she gave me her sweater and said she didn't care if I stretched it out wearing it, so we walked a little way down the steep slope to the first boulder.

"Limestone," said Felice, "that's the bedrock around here."

Felice had discovered her love of geology while doing a report on strip mining for a science class a couple of years back. She had picked the topic because of the soft-eyed deer that were featured in the oil company's commercials grazing on restored drilling sites, but she had gotten sidetracked by rocks.

She liked to touch them. Some rocks had sharp curves like the models in *Cosmo*. Some were porous and rough. Rocks were their own history, she said. She could tell if a rock was formed by fire or water or pressure just by holding it in her hand. Rocks were impartial and pretty much stayed put. Besides, there would be jobs for a petroleum geologist.

We scrambled onto the boulder and looked out over the pines. I picked at a gray growth in a crack.

"That's lichen. It takes years and years to grow. Don't pull it up." Felice's tone was sharp, but I had already broken it off.

"I didn't know." I shivered and scooted over closer to Felice. Pebbles bounced off under my foot. "I wish we had some pot."

We heard an owl. Felice shrugged. "Char," she said, "tell me something good."

"Like what?" I dropped the lichen into her lap.

She picked it up. "I don't know. I just want to hear something real good."

I slapped at a mosquito. "You're floating in chocolate syrup."

"That's disgusting. Too sticky." Felice looked out over the dark tops of the pines, toward another big boulder that was spray-painted with the word SUCK in blue.

I liked wearing her sweater, even though it didn't fit at all. It smelled like Felice. I got inspired. "Okay, you're in a mountain clearing. There's a lot of tiny flowers and grass. You're wearing a white lace dress. A stream is running, almost singing nearby. You bite a plum."

Felice stuck out her lip. "No food. Nothing fattening."

"All right, so you walk to the stream and take a sip of water, and it's cold on your tongue. It's also sweet, it's juicy like water from a plum, only it's cal-free." I had goosebumps on my arms, but I was starting to enjoy the spring chill.

Felice drummed the heels of her black Adidas on the rock. "Listen, am I by myself here? Isn't there anybody else around?"

"There will be. You hear someone coming through the forest—rustling noises." I reached down and stirred up some pine needles that had gathered in a depression in the boulder. They crackled.

Felice gave me an indulgent look. "Who is it?"

I said the first thing that came into my head. "It's me. I've got a white dress, too."

"You?" Felice looked at me, surprised.

"Me. We go barefoot in the water and sing Donna Summer songs, and the wind blows our skirts, and we're beautiful." The dark was coming on.

She took up the story. "It's sunny. We're drinking wine."

I nodded. "We laugh so hard we have to lean on each other, and we still fall down on the grass."

The wind picked up. Felice's hair blew back. "I do a dance," she said.

"You look strong. There's so much sun." My own hair was tickling my forehead.

"That sounds nice," Felice said as she rubbed the bit of lichen between her fingers, "but I'm getting cold. Let's go home."

SATURDAY, FELICE AND I had a double date at the Forever Drive-In. Mrs. Ventura insisted on helping me hot-comb my hair before we went out. Felice was spending an extra long time in the bathroom.

"You're very lucky, Charlotte. Some girls don't have legs." Mrs. Ventura flicked her finger at the fat under my chin. "You should be glad to be seeing this boy. He's not so ugly."

He was, though, ugly right through to his heart.

His name was Tim. He wasn't sweet or cute, but he sure was available. That was good enough for me. We were at the tail end of our romance, my first, which consisted of me picking him up from his job at the shoe store

and going for take-out fried chicken. He liked extra pack-
ets of catsup. He was eight years older than me, but he
lived with his mother and always wanted to park and
make out. We'd toss the bucket with the greasy napkins
and the chicken bones into the back so we could embrace
across the emergency brake. He was stiff-lipped and
abrupt. It was hard to get home without catsup stains on
my blouse.

Still, I liked the idea of having a boyfriend and I liked
being touched, at least the parts of me he did touch. He
acted as if my belly was a vast no-man's-land, which he
avoided at all costs, no matter how awkward that made
his grab for my breasts.

We broke up when he made a play for Felice. She told
me about it, of course. I asked him what was going on, and
he said I wasn't attractive enough to be faithful to. Just
like that. I left him off at the shoe store that afternoon with
a messy sense of relief. No more chicken filling the Pinto
with the smell of grease. He had hurt me, but that was
how I had expected things to work out, more or less.

BUT THAT WAS later. I was still seeing Tim when we
went to the drive-in that night. He had brought me a little
gift, some queen-sized anklet nylons that he had lifted
from work. Felice was with Mark, a freckle-faced over-
achiever from school.

Felice was good with men. She flirted. She dated. She
joked with the guy who pumped her gas, getting out of
the car to lean on the hood and pop her gum. She went
through guys fast, but her recklessness had a conserva-
tive edge. She drew the line.

Mark was following her around like a puppy, fetching
big cups of Tab and Eskimo Pies from the concession
stand, but I could tell he wouldn't last. For one thing, he

couldn't dance. Felice fidgeted all through the first feature, a cop action-comedy. She had to go to the bathroom in the middle of the big chase scene, so we took the long walk, threading through the parked cars to the dark line of doorless stalls where almost no one cared to linger, but Felice needed to do her lips and check her face in the small yellow mirror. I leaned on the browned sink, wondering if I had enough need and nerve to use one of those exposed toilets.

"My mother's been reading my mail again," Felice said as she tried to get the rusty faucet to work. "She slapped me when I called her a bitch."

"Felice, that's awful." I stared at her face in the mirror. She was smearing liquid foundation on her cheeks. "Are you okay?" I asked.

She shrugged and got out her mascara. "That's nothing. She set my blanket on fire once when I was a kid. On my bed. Burned a big hole in the mattress." Her lashes were getting thicker and blacker with every stroke. "I wasn't in the bed at the time."

Her eyes came out perfect. Felice had everything under control. Even the faucet started to work.

"You must have been really scared." My stomach always hurt when I was upset, and it was twisting inside of me now. I wanted to ask Felice why she had never told me about the fire, but that made me feel stuck on myself, so I said, "Why did she do it?"

Felice was tucking everything back into her disco bag. "I loved the blanket," she told me, putting the cap back on her lip gloss. "Mama said it was a bad habit."

The movie was over by the time we got back to the car, and another feature was about to come on. Mark must have climbed into the back seat while we were gone to share the last beer with Tim, because they were back there asleep, the two of them, snuggled against opposite sides of the car. Their mouths were identical, innocent O's, and they were both snorting softly as they slept.

Felice and I decided not to disturb them, so we unhooked the speaker from the window and carried it to the front of the car. We climbed up onto the hood, leaned back against the windshield, and cried our way through *The Other Side of the Mountain* out in the open night.

I GOT IT from Felice, my attraction for rocks. I fell in love with the word. It made me think of rock of ages, and rock and roll. It made me think of myself as a little girl lying in bed with my eyes closed, not moving at all, concentrating on rocking the bed, moving it in my mind. I was trying to get that swaying motion like a boat on the water, or a rocking horse, rocking myself to sleep, keeping at it until I felt my brain was swishing back and forth in my skull. I still did this sometimes, when I got home late from a night with Felice, too agitated to sleep.

I woke one morning with a buzz in my heart. I wanted to call Felice, but I knew better than to try that before eleven on a Saturday. I kicked off my blankets, stuck my feet in the air, and did the bicycle for five minutes. It was supposed to firm thighs. We did it every Monday, Wednesday, and Friday in P.E. I watched my thighs as I did it. They shook. I pinched one. Definitely not firm. I switched on the radio. Balmy. Unseasonable. Highs near seventy. It had been a hot spring. I put on my swimsuit and looked in the mirror. It was too small, but I found it kind of sexy. I wished there was someone who would appreciate me in it. Felice would tell me to burn it if she saw it. I picked up a handful of rocks from the nightstand. I didn't know their names. Felice would know—obsidian, feldspar, shale. She had a magnifying glass and a hardness chart. Something about whether a rock would scratch glass. It didn't matter. One crystal had a sharp edge, and I pulled it down my arm. It scratched me lightly.

It was 11:10 a.m. I daubed my arm with a Kleenex and called Felice.

"Felice."

"What?" Her voice was hoarse. She had started to smoke cigarettes, but only at parties.

"I woke up this morning with a buzz in my heart. Now it's moved to my stomach."

"A what?"

"My stomach is buzzing."

"Does it hurt?"

"It's crashing in there."

"Are you nauseous?"

"No, everything's kind of pulsing."

"Oh," said Felice. "That's just sex."

It wasn't just sex, though. I think it was life.

Chapter

Three

"FELICE."

"YEAH?"

"DO YOU WANT TO SPEND THE NIGHT AT MY house?" I was sitting crosslegged on the floor in her living room.

Felice was practicing a step in the reflection from the big window. She did a twirl and grabbed my shoulder to steady herself.

"God, I'm about as graceful as a cow in heat." She ran her fingers through her thick black hair.

I took a long drag on the pipe. "We could look at the stars. Use my mom's binoculars. See the moons of Jupiter," I said in a high, tight voice.

Felice tried the step again. This time it was perfect. She slid her hands down her body as a last touch, like the Pointer Sisters when they sang "Slow Hand."

"*The Man with the X-Ray Eyes* is on the late show. We could make nachos and watch it." I exhaled nice and slow.

"What about your parents?" Felice was still holding her pose.

"We'd be in the basement. They wouldn't bug us."

She danced around me to reach for the pipe. "You mean the moons of Jupiter are in your basement?"

She squatted down and blew smoke into my mouth. That was called a shotgun. I coughed. "Char. You're wasting it. Here, have some water."

My eyes were running. I could never smoke pot with the smooth elegance I felt when I first picked up the pipe. "Do you want to sleep over or not?"

"Do you have good hot water? I have to have a hot shower in the morning." She took another toke on the pipe, but couldn't get it to draw.

"Of course, we have great hot water." I poked the butt of a match into the ashes. Felice had never stayed over at my house when we were little. Her mother wouldn't let her sleep away from home.

She put her hand over the ashtray just when I was going to dump the pipe. "I think there's still a couple of hits left in there. All right. I'll come."

I balanced the pipe on the ashtray, careful that it didn't spill. "You will? That's great. It'll be fun. We'll tell ghost stories."

"I don't know any ghost stories." She made a ghoulish face, all droopy lips and teeth.

I started rolling up the baggie with the rest of the pot. "Do you want any more?" She shook her head. "Me neither. I have to get home before Mom gets off work. I'll see you tonight."

SHE SHOWED UP with a very full overnight case hanging from her shoulder and a sleeping bag beside her on the front step.

"Felice, you didn't need to bring that." I eyed the sleeping bag. "There's a double fold-out couch in the basement, right in front of the television." I had been making up the couch when the doorbell rang and had two pillows clutched in front of me.

Felice adjusted the strap on her overnight case and picked up the sleeping bag. "It's thermo-down fill. Good for temperatures of 30°F and below."

I motioned her inside and pulled the front door shut against the soft May night. "But it's warm. I've been sleeping naked every night." I whispered that last part, so Mom wouldn't hear me from the kitchen.

"Please, spare me," she said, making a face. She dropped the sleeping bag at the top of the stairs and gave it a nudge to send it bumping to the basement. "I borrowed that bag for this occasion and I intend to use it."

I threw both pillows down after it. "Maybe we can use it as a comforter to cover the couch."

Felice looked at me doubtfully. "Maybe."

"The basement floor is cold and hard." I gave her overnight case a little push to start it swinging from her shoulder.

"Careful. My blow dryer is in there."

We went downstairs.

"Girls," Mom called after us. "Dinner will be ready in about fifteen minutes. Would you like to come up and help me set the table?" We could barely hear her over the sound of popping grease.

"All right, all right. Give us a minute." I wanted to try to be nice to Mom in front of Felice. "We'll be right up."

"I brought the pot," Felice whispered. "Do you want to get high before supper?"

"She might smell it."

"Over all of those frying onions? I hate onions."

"I told her. She's cooking some of the meat separately for you."

"Good. I was afraid I wasn't going to be able to eat it. Are we going to get high or not?"

"It'll have to be quick."

"I know. I know." Felice was already getting out the baggie.

"Okay, how about in the bathroom? We can open the window and put a towel down across the bottom of the door." The whole idea made me tense.

Felice touched my arm. "Don't be so paranoid, Char. Come on."

We were red-faced and giggling at dinner, but the family was in a good mood so no one noticed. Mom had made hamburgers since I had a guest. She figured everyone loved hamburgers. It was true, too. Felice ate the whole thing, even her bun. Mom let me have a bun since it was Saturday night and all, but she herself stuck to eating a bare patty with one tablespoon of catsup and a celery stick. Jeff and Dad both had two burgers each, of course, with Fritos. Felice and I grabbed some chips, too. We were having a reckless night.

Felice told me that she liked looking at my family around the table, holding our burgers with both hands, peering over them at each other with our matching blue eyes. Mom and I were fat, Dad and Jeff were thin. Dad and I had brown hair. Jeff and Mom were blond. We all ate fast, and Felice said we all smelled like the same soap. We used Dial.

After dinner, Mom and Dad went to a movie with the Gerbers from across the street. Jeff took off with his friends. Felice had brought some of her records, so we went down to the basement and turned the stereo up loud. We practiced a few steps together until her favorite song came on. Then I sat on the arm of the couch and watched her as she danced on the slippery tile. She lip synced, moving her mouth, humming, sometimes coming in on a high note, pulling it out of herself. She closed her eyes. I thought she moved like a star, all success and real joy. She sang through the rest of the album. Sometimes she forgot the words, but she didn't seem to need them as much as the beat and the habit, the reassurance that this verse came after this version of the chorus, that this time the singer gave a long sigh after "love" and before "you." The sigh *was* the song. It made me shiver. I thought it held the weight of all of Felice's ambitions and desires, but she didn't freeze there. She did a long slow shimmy that ended with her crouched down to the tiles, then she kicked out her feet and dropped for the end of the song.

I clapped from the arm of the couch. "A star is born."

Felice jumped up and grabbed my hand. "Let's work on our dance steps." She put on *The Rocky Horror Picture Show.* I loved the record, but I wouldn't buy it because I was too embarrassed about the pictures on the album cover: hands on Janet's bra-cupped breasts and men in makeup might tell Mom something, if she saw it. Mom didn't usually pay much attention to records, though. She believed in books. She sat on the couch and breathed them in, sort of the way Felice breathed songs.

We danced through three more records before going outside to look at the stars. I could hear the hiss of a neighbor's sprinkler. The Big Dipper was easy to find, but that was as far as we got. I picked out a brightness that I decided was Jupiter, but I couldn't focus enough to find the moons.

We gave up and went back inside. It was getting late. Mom and Dad came in and called down the stairs, "Goodnight, girls. Be sure you get enough sleep." *The Man with the X-Ray Eyes* opened with a creepy shot of eyeballs with full roots bobbing in a jar. We decided that it was too gross to waste our time on, so we played a game of Scrabble. I won with triple points for the "z" in "zen."

Felice went into the bathroom to take out her contacts. I could hear her splashing water and humming. I called through the door, "Are you still sleeping on the floor?"

She opened the door. "What?" She was wearing blue-striped PJs that looked like long underwear, only flashier. I had changed into my sleeping t-shirt and clean underpants.

"Do you still want to roll your bag out on the floor, or should we use it as a comforter on the bed?" I felt odd, as if I were making a big deal out of something I'd be better off not mentioning.

"I'll use it on the bed," she said, smoothly, shortly. "But I'm not sleepy yet."

"You're not?" I was, but I wanted to savor every minute of the night more than I wanted to sleep.

"No." She came out of the bathroom with a bunch of little bottles and *Vogue* magazine. Did she look at the Before pictures once she had stripped her face? Did the glossy pages have special cleansing powers, like newspapers on car windows? I didn't ask.

"Maybe I'll read a while," she said.

"Me, too." So we unfolded the couch bed and stretched out on top of the blankets with the sleeping bag unzipped and thrown across for warmth. It was always cool in the basement, even in summer. I got out my copy of *Wuthering Heights,* but I kept letting it rest to look over Felice's shoulder at the bright ads full of thin, wild women. I admired the red mouths, the aura of sexiness and wealth. Felice paid close attention to the specific bits of clothing: shoes with straps; big, flat buttons; skirts slit to the hip.

"I could never walk down the streets of this town in that, but her hair is cute." Our faces were close over the pages. She poked her finger into one of the snarls in my own long, brown hair. "You should try to get yours under control."

I loved my hair. It was one of my secret vanities. Sometimes at night I would spread it out on my pillow. That felt like something only a beauty was supposed to do. But I could sneak into the sensual on its soft waves. Sometimes I chewed it. I worked the snarls with my fingers, trying to loosen the tiny knots, but I just combed over the top of them when I went out into the world. They felt hidden enough against my neck. Mom bought me barrettes and pony tail ties, but I only pulled it back if I felt very pious, like at church or on a date. My glasses kept it out of my eyes most of the time.

Felice was one for radical changes of style, from little fringes to smooth buns to short perms. She had mentioned my hair problem to me before.

I gave her the answer I always gave. "Would you fix it for me?"

She was looking at a page where the model in the sparse macrame swimsuit had her hair slicked back into a pompadour. Felice stretched out a little more on the bed. "I'm too tired."

I flipped to an ad. "Oh, come on. Here's your chance. Before/After."

She rolled onto her side. "Please, Char. If I had a chance to Before/After anyone, it would be me."

I kicked off the sleeping bag. "Really, Felice. I could get Mom's sewing scissors. She keeps them down here."

She sat up. "God, no. No scissors. I can't handle the responsibility. You've been growing that hair for years."

"I've had it cut before. At my grandmother's in Iowa when I was in the fourth grade. Remember?" I went into an all-out wheedle. "Come on, Felice. *Please.*"

She groaned. "Enough, enough." She grabbed my chin and looked me full in the face. "Okay, I'll see what I can do."

My stomach dropped. "You sure you're not too tired?" I wanted the attention, but I also liked being able to drop my hair around my face. It did something powerful for me, even if I wasn't sure what.

"What's the problem? A minute ago you were begging me to do it. Where are the scissors?" Her tone was brisk.

"I just meant a new style. I didn't mean you actually had to cut it." I couldn't believe I had gotten myself into this.

Felice sighed. "Make up your mind. You've got exactly three seconds before I forget the whole thing and go to sleep annoyed."

"That's quite a threat." I was stalling. "Haven't you ever had second thoughts?"

"One thousand one, one thousand two. . ."

"All right, I have an idea. Why don't you French braid it? That will get it under control, and I can think about whether I really want to lose it altogether."

Felice made a face. "Braiding is boring." She poked the snarl again. "Still, it would help. And if you pay attention, you can learn how to do it yourself."

I held my head under the bathroom faucet. She gave me a shampoo and creme rinse. We sat on the bed in front of an old movie about a woman with an incurable disease who had no way of knowing when it would strike again. Felice combed out the snarls. The star had decided to go ahead and take a chance on love by the time Felice was satisfied. Felice divided the hair into even strands and began to braid.

I felt the pull at my roots as she wove a little more into her pattern with every crossed strand. I closed my eyes and leaned back against her, but she said that made it too hard to work, so I sat up straight as she knelt behind me. I felt her breath. Her fingers brushed my neck. Every now and then she took my face in her hands and held my head straight. She needed to be sure that the braids were even. She smelled like pot and strawberry shampoo. I could hear the brush of flannel as she moved. Her knees rested against the soft spread of my back. My face was being tugged out into the air.

She finished. There was a sofa-and-loveseat commercial on. She put down the comb and leaned across me to get a look from the front. I felt my face turning red. She put her arms around me, and we kissed. It was soft. Our tongues touched. I heard the heroine saying, "Oh, John, this *is* the rest of my life."

We both started laughing at the same time. I hugged her, then let her go so she could untangle her legs. I was sitting on the comb. She stroked my neck. I moved my hand over her flannel sides. The credits were rolling on the small screen. She was playing with my braids.

I got up to turn the television off. When I came back to the bed, everything had changed.

Felice was wrapping the sleeping bag around her, zipping it up as she went. I sat close to her and touched the arm that was still out there doing the zipping. She was staring intently at a place where the nylon had snagged in the teeth, working it back and forth.

"Felice."

"Huh?"

I didn't know what to say. "Are you cold? We've got extra blankets."

She freed the snag and pulled in her arm. "No, I'm fine. Just sleepy."

I knew I couldn't sleep. "Look, Felice, can we talk about this for a minute?" I pulled on the drawstring of her bag.

"Cut it out. That makes it tighter."

"Sorry." I stopped.

"It's all right." She turned her blue cocoon back to me.

"So, can we talk?"

"Talk about what?" I had heard her voice this flat before, when she was telling her mother she was going out.

"About, about all this." I shook my head a little and the braids swung back and forth.

"They look very nice," she said into the mattress.

"Felice, talk to me." I found her shoulder through the nylon.

She looked up. "Don't press me, Char. You're always pressing me."

She was right. I had kind of forced her into doing my hair. I always begged favors out of her like that. Well, if this was what a favor felt like, I could do without it. I looked down at my paunch pushing up under my t-shirt as I sat crosslegged on the blankets.

I felt bitter and stupid. Felice had been feeling sorry for me, and it had gone too far.

"Char. Char." She sounded urgent in her bag. "Let's just go to sleep, okay? I'm sorry. I just don't want to talk about anything."

I turned out the light. "Okay." I got under the covers and curled tight, pressing my forehead into the hard arm of the couch. I cried into the upholstry for a while before giving in to sleep to pass the night.

WE WOKE IN the morning to the rattle of the dish-washer in the kitchen upstairs. Felice had a grumpy morning squint to her eyes. It was strange to get this kind of look at her.

"God, I need coffee," she said, sitting up in her sleeping bag.

I yawned. We got dressed and went up for breakfast, but I had coolness in my heart. Last night had also iced up my brain stem. My problems felt that easy to locate, although there were other things hidden, solid and motionless in the general freeze.

I was reading the back of the Fruit Loops box. Felice pulled a piece of paper out of her disco purse and studied it as she ate dry toast.

"What's that?" I asked, fishing in my bowl for Fruit Loops.

Felice was removing her crusts. "A hardness chart. We can go try to identify rocks in the mountains tomorrow."

"You know I'm lousy at identification. I just like rocks."

She took a sip of Tang. "You have to be able to tell sandstone from basalt before you can say anything else about them."

I slurped some sugary milk from my spoon. "I'm still trying to figure out whether I'm animal, vegetable, or mineral, myself."

Felice put down her chart. "It's too early in the morning for quests."

Jeff wandered in wearing sweatpants and a tight white t-shirt. He sat down at the table with his box of Life and said, "Hi, girls."

His eyes were puffed up from whatever he had been doing the night before, and he smelled sweaty from his morning run. He picked up his spoon and flipped some cereal at me, but it missed me by a mile.

"Grow up," said Felice, but she was giving him a grin.

Mom came in wearing her green velour robe. "Oh, good, I wanted to be sure you kids were eating breakfast. Charlotte, those braids are very becoming. You must have lost some weight yesterday. Does anybody want grapefruit? There's some on the bottom shelf of the refrigerator." She wasn't eating anything herself.

"No, thanks."

"No, thanks." Jeff kept reading the funnies over Felice's shoulder while we were eating. I felt sick.

Felice packed up her stuff. I helped her get it all out to her car, then stood next to her window as she settled the sleeping bag and the overnight case into the back seat.

"Thanks for coming." I rubbed something squashed from her windshield with my sleeve. It smeared, and my sweatshirt came back dirty.

Felice fastened her seatbelt. "Yeah. It was fun."

I tried to wipe my sleeve on my jeans. "God, wasn't that one dying starlet movie stupid." I was looking at the stain.

Felice switched the radio on. "Just awful," she said. Then she drove away.

I pushed a strand of hair behind one ear. My braids were already starting to come loose.

MOM CAME INTO my room that afternoon. She knocked on my door and opened it at the same time. I was sitting on my bed with the small pile of rocks from my nightstand. They were gathered in a sunken place in the mattress, and I was rolling them around there under my palm.

Mom gave me a nervous smile. "Hi. What are you doing?"

"Reinventing the wheel. Could you please wait until I say 'Come in' before you walk into my room? There's no point in knocking if you don't wait." I didn't like the expression on my face, even from the inside.

Mom decided not to take it personally this time. "All right. I'm sorry." She sat down next to me on the bed. The rocks shifted toward her weight. "I just wanted to know if you wanted to go swimming with me. It's part of the diet."

"Right now?"

"Yes. I just have to get my swimsuit on."

"Okay." I couldn't read or talk. Swimming might help, if I could survive the locker room.

I was ready before she had changed and found her keys. We both wore our suits under our street clothes. The suits were the same tank style, mine black, hers navy blue.

In the car on the drive to the gym, she said, "You look tired." She was talking to the rearview mirror.

I answered her cheek. "Yeah, we stayed up late."

"Did you find the moons of Jupiter?"

"Sure. It was really something." I lied out of habit, and because I wasn't sure about anything that had happened last night. When in doubt, make it sound nice.

"That's great. What did they look like?" She pulled into the parking lot.

"They were very small, dark circles passing in front of the light from the planet."

"Really? They were dark?" She got out. "Maybe you can show me sometime."

I grabbed the towels and the shampoo. "Sure. Any time."

In the locker room, Mom and I were like two dark balloons at a skinny girls' parade. They watched us with covert looks, suspicious of themselves, suspicious that some part of our bodies might suggest some part of theirs. We armed ourselves with the small white towels that we had been handed at the desk and proceeded to the pool.

I swam one length, then stopped and looked across at Mom. There were not many people in the pool, so we each had taken a lane of our own. She looked sort of silly, dog paddling in her bulky white cap. I didn't want to think about how I looked. I pushed off and swam back across. A man dove in, and he was soon on my heels, so I didn't pause at the wall that lap, but pushed off right away. I rushed through the next length, wondering why I hadn't stopped and moved aside to let him get in front of me at the other end. I hurried to the wall and let him pass. I looked over at Mom again. She looked completely absorbed, and her cap was slipping forward onto her face. She never put her head in. She was like a very young duck, surprised to feel at home in the water.

The Beach Boys were playing over the intercom. "Fun fun fun" echoed in my head, three funs for each stroke. The guy I had let pass before was trying to lap me again. I paused a moment to let him by, feeling very big and in his way. I wanted to keep my rhythm, so I kicked off again right behind him. I was irritated at having to keep adjusting my pace around him, but I also felt safe, covered and held by the water. I slipped into thinking about Felice. That burned some, like chlorine in my eyes. It made me feel loose and tight at the same time, like my body in the suit. Felice swam the same way she danced, for pleasure and speed. I thought of her skittering like a waterbug across the pond we had found in a remote part of Tuckers Park. She liked to move as much as she could, until she reached some kind of clear, empty exhaustion.

She always wanted to keep walking through the forest instead of standing like I did, facing trees and light.

"I'm more vegetable than animal," I thought. I rolled over on my back to float like a wet, black log.

This time Mr. Speedo splashed water in my face as he passed me, so when I reached the wall, I floated into the corner, and decided to wait a few rounds out.

Mom was alone in her lane. It might have been thinking about Felice that let me notice how good Mom looked in the water, but once I finally saw her beauty, it seemed ordinary and familiar. Mom seemed to wake up in the water. She was so loose and white, buoyed up by her fat. She could rest at the surface and make little dips with her hands and feet. I knew she was happy in the pool in a way she wouldn't be in a pond. She liked knowing where the edges were. I watched her bump against the floats strung along the blue rope that marked her lane.

Mr. Afternoon Olympics, finally finished, climbed out of the pool, his own personal shag carpet dripping from his chest. I tugged my swimsuit down and started another slow lap, keeping my head in, waiting as long as I could to come up for breath, staring into the sharp blue bottom of the pool.

When we got out, I handed Mom her towel. "You looked good in there."

She winced. "I'm surprised that you're willing to be seen with me."

We moved quickly out of the yellow-green light, pulling our towels as far as they would go around our waists.

Chapter Four

I DROVE TO FELICE'S THE NEXT DAY TO PICK her up so we could go to the mountains. It was a warm spring afternoon. The sunshine was pale as a lemon drop. All the lawns along her street were coming into their first tender green. There was a big hole in Felice's front yard. Her father had tried to plant a tree, but it died. The hole was very brown in the middle of all that green.

I knocked on the heavy wooden front door, but there was no answer. I knocked again, then turned the knob and stuck my head in, calling hello. I heard voices coming from the kitchen, so I stepped into the hallway. I heard Mrs. Ventura shouting. I stood still.

"Stop it, Mama. Leave me alone." Felice sounded much younger than usual and a little afraid.

Her mother got louder. "You won't care when I'm dead."

I turned back to the door and opened it softly, then stepped outside and started ringing the bell. I had to lean on it hard and long before anyone answered. Felice came to the door with a dark stain on her shirt, reeking of lemon ammonia. I stared at her.

"Hi, Char." She seemed calm, if a little annoyed. "I was helping Mama clean, and she spilled stuff on me. I have to change. I'll just be a minute."

Felice held the door open. I stayed where I was. I wanted her to whisper something nasty about her mother the bitch. "Well, come on in," she said.

"I'll wait here." I sat down on the step. "It's so nice out." I was scared to see Mrs. Ventura furious and scared to see her calm. It was weird enough to watch Felice wearing her most ordinary face, with just a small chip of anger in her eye. She went back inside.

Some early bees were working Mrs. Peterson's flowers. One was stumbling around and around in the grass near a petunia. I could hear the water running in the house.

Felice came back out, and we drove into the mountains. She was nervous on the narrow, winding road. I didn't say anything about her mother. The Pinto set its own pace, which was slow. Jeeps kept passing us on the hairpin curves. Felice was trying to count back to Precambrian times in the layers of rock in the cliff that rose on one side of us. The other side was a sheer drop to the river. I started singing old Girl Scout songs, but Felice had never been a scout, so we did everything we knew from *Jesus Christ, Superstar* instead.

We parked at a wide spot on the river that was just a gentle slope down from the road. There were a couple of picnic tables, and the current seemed slow enough for wading. The sun was so fresh I could smell it. It smelled like Felice.

We waded across the cold river, climbed out, and started to hike. Felice bent down. I looked at her back. She picked up a dust-colored rock, saying that the dust itself was millions of specks of this very rock. It made me queasy to think of something that hard ground down until it was scattered and soft. I scrounged up a palmful of dirt, which I knew was a thin coating over the layers of limestone and granite. The dirt felt dry and light and had a sharp, almost salt smell that rock didn't have.

I held out my hand to Felice. "Here, smell the dirt."

She took a pinch and held it near her nose. "That might be the actinomycetes. They're kind of like a fungus. They break down the rock. Maybe they smell." She opened her fingers and lost her pinch. "You're getting it all over your face," she said to me.

I wiped my face with the back of my hand. It felt gritty. I imagined small bits of rock slipping into me through my pores, into my veins, so that the dust started to circulate, spreading through me like oxygen, riding my blood. It had to happen all the time. Inorganic things came into me with my air, with my food, through my skin, and lived my life. I must be mineral, I thought, playing my game.

Felice tasted her rock. "Granite," she said.

We both looked down. I saw trampled grass, dust, a six-pack plastic. She saw something else.

"No, gneiss," she said, rubbing the chunk with her nail. "Let's look for something pure."

She walked staring at the ground, sometimes crouching and scratching, until we came to an outcropping of boulders. Felice started to climb without even stopping for breath. I tried to follow, scrambling up, squeezing through tight places that were easy for her, willing my arms to lift the rest of me up over a ledge. She stayed ahead, kicking gravel down, even though she kept stopping to peer into cracks. I liked the climbing, the air, the cold rock against my legs. I just didn't like the pace. But Felice kept moving, chipping off specimens, putting them in baggies, and making labels for them. She had an alertness all over her, a kind of listening tilt, as if the stones should speak.

I reached up to grab a handhold, and a lump of rock came off under the pressure of my fingers. I wobbled a little but kept my footing. I looked at the rock. It was shiny. I called to Felice. She turned around and held up her hands, so I tossed it up to her. It was a sloppy throw. I gasped as she reached to catch it, but she was stable as always. She scratched it with her thumbnail, sending a small shower of gold flakes down on my head.

"Pyrite," she called. "Fool's gold." She dropped it into the pocket of her shorts, already bulging, and turned to continue to climb.

I started back down. It was enough. I banged up my bare legs a little more, then found a flat place a little way from the base of the boulders, where I could lie in the sun listening to the river and watching Felice climb.

Her blue t-shirt stood out against the pink rock, but it dulled when she was outlined against the brighter blue of the sky. Felice gathered rocks like they were stars. She knew that there were so many of them that she'd never have one of each, but she could group them, arrange them in ground-level constellations, and find her direction by the mountain piles of them in the west. Felice wasn't after the myths that usually went with constellations, though. She wanted to get a grip on the facts. That was hard since even the stars were constantly moving, and there was a tumult of magma under the earth's thin crust.

If I hadn't heard it, I never would have guessed Felice had just had a fight with her mother. She didn't seem upset. She just kept working: compiling data and making field observations. I admired that detachment in her, even though it scared me a little. I watched her on the boulders, hefting a stone in her palm, trying its weight. I saw her take aim at the trunk of a tree. A bird flew out of a hole in the bark with a rush of wings, disturbed by the thud.

THERE'S ALWAYS A Pizza Hut in any small mountain town, so we stopped and drank watery beer from red plastic pitchers in Grantler on the way home. I complained because Ponderosa Steak House and K-Mart had turned me down for summer jobs. Felice squared her shoulders to make fun of two men in business suits knocking off a large pepperoni across the room. They gave her a couple of measuring looks, and when we ordered another pitcher, I got the feeling that they were keeping track. I thought that they were only looking at Felice without taking notice of me at all, but I was wrong.

Felice's face was flushed with beer and sun. Her knees kept bumping mine under the table. She dug a quarter out of her pocket to play a Blondie song on the table jukebox. I poured her another beer. She emptied the rocks out of her pockets onto the table, looking for more change.

She was talking fast. "It's about checking things out, Char. You establish a premise, then you try to find out if it's true."

I cocked my head at her. "So, how do you find out?"

She blew into the foam. "You gather data." She sipped. "You explore facts."

I cleaned out my fingernail with a fork. "You're so cautious."

Her face got very still, although she laughed when she said, "You think so? I feel kind of wild. Like I wouldn't mind going home with a businessman tonight. I could tell Mama I was sleeping over at your house."

I started tapping the rim of my glass with the fork. "What if she calls?"

Felice laughed again. "Tell her to go burn some of my clothes or something." She reached over and took my fork. "Don't. Anyway, I'm just talking. We haven't even met those guys."

The beer hit me. I told Felice I had to pee and walked up toward the counter where the bathrooms were. I felt like I was walking through an avalanche zone.

I was. One of the business suit men, the older, stiffer one, passed me in the narrow hall to the bathroom with his briefcase under his arm. He stopped and let a slow smile work his mouth.

"Pig ass," he muttered, much too close to my ear. "Fat one. Fatso. Fat ass." His voice was cool and soft.

I stood frozen for a moment, then tried the door to the women's room. It was locked. "Pig ass." He grinned. "Hey, fatty." He was blocking my way out of the hall. I wanted to knock him over and kick his face in. I had on sensible shoes. His identifying bones would crack.

The door to the women's room opened and the woman who had been working behind the counter came out. She must have heard at least his last couple of words, but she had a polite, neutral look on her face. I ducked into the bathroom behind her and locked the door, breathing hard. I sat on the toilet and put both hands flat on the walls. The businessman and his friend were gone by the time I came out.

Felice had put another quarter in the table jukebox, and sat listening to the music and fingering her rocks.

She was singing under her breath, "Sweeeet, sweet, sweet," along with the song.

I sat down and picked up my mug of beer.

"That'll be flat by now," she said, nodding at the beer. "Your eyes look red."

"One of those business guys started calling me names." I took a sip anyway. She was right—flat.

Felice put her cool hand out and covered my hot one on the table. "Stupid shit. What kind of names?"

I shrugged, not looking at her, but glad she had touched me. "The usual. Fat."

"Oh." She took the glass out of my other hand and leaned toward me. I was conscious of my stomach pressing against the table on my side of the booth. I started to cry. She reached across the table and took off my glasses, then wiped my cheeks with a paper napkin. I shuddered. She rubbed the back of her hand across my soft chin. I was shaking, but she was the one who dropped the glass.

Beer splattered everywhere. "I'm sorry, Char," she said. We mopped it up. The glass cracked clean and kept its shape, but I couldn't trust it to drink from after that.

ON THE DRIVE home, Felice said, "I've been thinking about my mother."

I was still cloudy-headed and a little nauseous, trying to concentrate on steering, but I managed a nod.

Felice said something else that I missed, then she tugged on the hem of my shorts. I took my foot off the gas and turned to look at her. She was making a point.

"Char, I want us to be stable. I want you to be my best friend, right out of 'Laverne and Shirley'." I snorted, but she persisted. "Promise."

I looked back at the road and gave in. "Of course, yeah, you know I care about you," I said. I knew what I was promising. I moved my leg away from her hand.

Then Felice told me that she was going to stay with her cousin Mickey and Mickey's husband Rick in New Mexico for the summer. She said that she could get restaurant work there, for sure, and she wanted to get a good look at some geological structures—mesas and buttes and dormant volcanoes.

I didn't know I was furious until I had driven all the way down from the mountains and dropped Felice off at her house. After she shut her front door, I slammed my fist into the turn signal. It lit up green on the dashboard. I hit it again, and the switch snapped off. I threw it out of the window as hard as I could. It landed in Mrs. Peterson's garden, right in the middle of her petunias.

I had to give hand signals the rest of the way home.

A FEW DAYS later Mom was cleaning up after the dog in the backyard. I was following her around holding a grocery sack for her to dump the turds into when I said, "Felice is going to New Mexico for the summer."

Mom was swift and efficient with her metal scoop. "What does Felice's mother think about that?"

I just opened my mouth and told her what I figured. It felt odd. "She thinks Felice is trying to get away from her."

The dog was watching us from a corner of the yard, looking sheepish.

"That's what happens when girls are seventeen," said Mom.

There was a crash. The dog had knocked over the trash. He did it out of embarrassment at having so much attention paid to his messes, I thought.

Chapter

Five

ON THE FIRST DAY OF MY SUMMER JOB, I found myself mopping up eggs and cake from the floor of the nursing home, trying not to stain my new uniform. Felice was gone.

My hands had been sweaty when I filled out the application and I hadn't been able to remember the address of my elementary school, but the nursing home had given me the job anyway. They paid four dollars an hour, which was fifty cents more than Taco Bell was paying that summer. Mom bought me two white polyester pantsuits and some soft-soled shoes.

I was a nurse's aide. I was supposed to lift people and dress them and bathe them and feed them. It sounded hard, but I figured I could give them my four dollars' worth.

I drove to work along the same route that Felice and I had cruised so many times that spring, down Moody

Boulevard past the Lucky U Motel and Jack in the Box. I thought of her as I pulled into the parking lot, but then I thought about her almost all of the time. She'd been gone two weeks, and I hadn't heard a word.

Another aide named Perez was assigned to train me my first day. She was calm and friendly, and she rode her linen cart down the hall like it was a skate board. I had to trot to keep up, nervous about banging into somebody's wheelchair. She made her beds like she wore her uniform: crisp and tight. I spent fifteen minutes on one bed, trying to get the corners of the sheet to square off right. Perez came over and finished it for me. "You'll get it," she said, tucking back a wisp of hair that had fallen out of her braid. "Why don't you finish these last two rooms by yourself, then meet me at lunch."

As I walked down the long hall to the cafeteria, I could hear the clatter of dishes and smell steamed meat. I pushed open the big double doors and looked around for Perez. I was standing next to the dish window where folks brought their trays after they finished eating. There were old people clustered around every table and lined up along the walls with trays on their wheelchairs. The meal was meatloaf, corn, white bread, and yellow cake with pink frosting. I was supposed to feed it to people, but I couldn't imagine how I was going to reach across the gap between me and a stranger and put a spoon in their mouth. Perez had to teach me. I felt worse than I did at school lunch when I had no one to sit with.

Finally, I spotted Perez sitting on the edge of a table, her uniform looking impossibly elegant even at this distance. She was leaning over a black-haired woman in a wheelchair, speaking earnestly into her ear. They both laughed. Perez gestured with a spoon above the woman's plate, but nobody at that table seemed to be eating. The woman jerked her head toward the spoon, and Perez put it down.

Another patient, a woman with gray hair, pulled away from their table. She was waving a slice of bread speared on a fork in front of her. I couldn't really see her face, but I noticed how strong her hands were, and how fast she was moving across the floor. She wheeled up to the dish window and said, "May I have this toasted?" Her voice was high and sweet.

I noticed the woman Perez had been talking with coming across the floor, too. The kitchen aide, up to her elbows in greasy dishwater, said, "No, we don't do toast."

"Toast," the bread woman said again. She practically sang it. "I want this toasted!"

"No," said the aide impatiently, turning away, so the bread woman drove her chair at the counter, bent her head, and butted the pan of dishwater onto the floor. The aide jumped back from the slap of water. Before I could think how to react, Perez's friend pushed past me, straight into the swinging doors of the kitchen. She stopped, propping the doors open with her chair. She was right beside me, so I got a good look at her stiff red face and her blue eyes, one of which stared out across the crowd and one of which seemed to slide over me.

She yelled something in a low rough voice. I couldn't quite understand her, but I thought she said something about a salad bar. She scooped up her lump of meatloaf from her chair tray and held it in the air. Her whole arm seemed to vibrate. I stood there staring at her shaking arm and her curled red fist holding the brown meat, then watched her sling it to the floor. I stepped back. It slid across the tiles into the kitchen right to the feet of the approaching head cook. The bread woman swung her fork and threw the bread after it. Old women were surging into the kitchen, and I backed away from the door.

I felt as if I was watching a late-night movie. Everywhere I looked I saw something strange. A woman in a blue-flowered house dress punched a hole in a bag of flour with her cane, dusting herself with white. The cook was struggling with the bread woman for possession of a loaf, and I stared at their hands: long skinny fingers and big knuckles with the skin stretched tight across them versus short sturdy hands shiny with cooking burns across their backs. The meatloaf woman was at a counter cracking eggs with her elbows. Next to her, a middle-aged woman with caramel-colored skin and violet shoes rolled her chair over squares of cake. Old women were knocking huge pots of gravy from the stove to the floor. There were bursts of light, as if flashbulbs were going off, but I couldn't tell who was taking pictures. I looked back into the cafeteria and saw Perez laughing. She tossed a hot-dog bun at me, but it bounced off my knee. Men in their shirt sleeves came in from the offices and stood on the edge of the crowd with their arms crossed. A bald one carried a Burger King bag. The cook was trying to get aides to start wheeling folks away. She grabbed my arm and pushed me out toward the tables. "Get them back to their rooms," she said.

I walked up to a man who had his head down on the table. His neck was wrinkled in hundreds of tiny folds, and his pink scalp shone through his soft, white hair. He was sleeping through the riot. I lifted his shoulders to help him sit up in his chair, and his eyelids fluttered, but he didn't open them. The woman sitting next to him was taking food off his tray and hiding it in her lap. "Mr. Pierson never eats a bite," she told me, folding a napkin over her thighs. I wheeled Mr. Pierson back to the wing and left him, breathing gently, next to a bed.

Perez had been mustered to wheel folks away, too. I never saw anyone walk so slow as she did on her way to get the woman with the violet shoes who was crushing cakes. Perez offered a courtly bow and wiped pink frosting off the wheels with a napkin. The woman gave her a smile so bright that the meatloaf woman turned and stared at the two of them.

Later, I caught up with Perez, who was standing outside of the room where she had left Violet Shoes, listening to the slow song that was coming from inside. She burst out laughing when she saw the look on my face. "Don't worry, chica, it's not like this every day." She called over my shoulder. "Hey, Peg, here's someone who needs a little education."

Peg turned out to be the meatloaf woman, her long black hair white with flour, gravy splashed up the legs of her sweat pants. She headed her chair for Perez and stopped just short of running her over. "Can you believe it?" Her voice was low and rough, but if I concentrated I could understand her. "I never imagined anything so good. There was a reporter there, you know."

Perez gave her a small punch on the arm. "Yeah, taking pictures. I noticed. It was really something, Peg. I just hope there's not too much trouble over it. Here, let me give Char one of those flyers, then I'll take the rest and get rid of them for you."

Peg looked at me and nodded, so Perez reached for the stack of paper that was jammed under the cushion of Peg's chair. She gave me one and folded the rest into the pocket of her tunic. Her uniform was still immaculate.

Peg turned her chair into the doorway of Violet Shoes' room. The record player was crooning something tender. I recognized Sam Cooke from my dad's stack of old records. With a mock romantic sigh, Perez handed me a mop. "Ginny's room, where it's always the fifties." She gave me a little push in the direction of the cafeteria. "You'd better help clean up." I set off in that direction, but I stopped before I'd gone very far to read the flyer. It was a call to action:

Tired of gray meat and white bread?
Tired of vegetables so over-cooked they
puddle on your plate?
Tired of warm orange juice and cold coffee,
of tasteless meals with no choice about
what you're eating or how it's prepared?
Let the people in charge know we want some
control over what we eat.
Demand a salad bar.
TIME FOR A FOOD STRIKE.
BOYCOTT LUNCH...

The next day there was an article on page one of the Moody paper, with a big photo of Mr. Pierson sleeping with his head on the table, while a hunk of meatloaf flew past. I considered the caption: "Oldsters protest food at nursing home."

Mom read sections of the article aloud to me over breakfast. They quoted a Mrs. Eugenia Cribbs as saying, "I think they planned a peaceful protest that got out of hand. I don't approve of the method, but I do not think a salad bar is too much to ask."

Mom lowered the paper and looked at me. "She's got a point. Every Furr's Cafeteria has one."

I nodded and reached into the cupboard for some Carnation Instant Breakfast. As I was stirring the powder into the milk, the doorbell rang. Mom went to answer it, and I had to look twice, because for a moment I thought that her beige sandals were leaving smudges of Velveeta on the floor, as if she had been stomping the cheese. But the dog walked out behind her without licking her footprints, so they must have just been puddles of light.

AFTER THE FOOD fight, word went out that the front office wanted the names of the people who had been involved. Everyone knew Peg was already at the top of the list. There would have been trouble, except that the newspaper article brought a small blizzard of phone calls, some crates of lettuce, and some uncomfortable attention from the Board of Health. The bald Mr. John Jonas from the front office actually appeared on the wing. He met with Peg, Ginny, and Mrs. Eugenia Cribbs, who turned out to be the woman I had seen puncturing sacks of flour. They became the Food Committee.

"What about the woman who spilled the dishwater?" I asked Perez. "Looked to me like she started the whole thing."

Perez patted my cheek. "Oh, you haven't met Iris yet, have you? Nobody has meetings with Iris." I found out later that Iris was riot-furious all the time.

The committee achieved a salad bar, complete with sunflower seeds and three kinds of dressing. Peg was ecstatic and took to writing regular letters to the editor about conditions in the home. She got letters back, too. I saw them on her bedside table.

I noticed the letters because Peg didn't have anybody who came in from outside. There was only one picture on her bedside table: a group shot of a bunch of firemen with a dark-haired woman doing a showgirl kick in firemen's boots. Her roommate Mabel's side of the room was covered with old photographs in big gilt frames. Peg found her friends on the wing.

She spent a lot of time in Ginny's room, taking notes with a pencil strapped to her wrist. She was writing an exposé of the nursing home. Ginny had framed prints on her walls. She even had her own sheets and a red comforter, which meant that she had to have people from outside do her laundry because the nursing home wouldn't. Her sisters came in for it, most often a thin elegant woman named Lilah. Lilah would stride up the hall bringing Ginny a pair of emerald green sandals from her husband's shoe factory and stride away with a bag of Ginny's dirty clothes.

Sometimes Lilah's little boy came with her, carrying a record album he had picked out himself from the oldies bin. Ginny would give him some change from a bag she kept tucked into the seat of her chair, and he would run to the common room to get a Pepsi for his mother and an orange drink for himself from the machine. He was twitchy, and Ginny liked to keep him busy, so he wouldn't pull leaves off her plants or spill orange soda out the window.

WHEN I GOT home from work one night, there was a letter from Felice:

> Dear Char,
>
> Got a job in a truckstop. Hot dishwater in the backroom, and my face is breaking out from so much pop and grease. Still, I have days off to get out into the hills. I think about you when I'm driving. I drive a lot. My car window arm is sunburnt. There's a small dormant volcano nearby, and a bigger one about four hours from here that I'd like to go to sometime. This little neighborhood volcano was serious when she went off. She changed everything for the plants and animals and people around here. It's a pumice world. One big breast hill. Tourists drive up it to picnic, if they feel like going so far off the highway.

Mostly it's local people. Kids from Mesquite High circle the rim, might as well be you and me. I haven't met anybody, but I hear their radios when they roll their windows down. Last night I had off work, so I parked by the side of the road and walked around the top. I kept trying to find the big bear in the sky, but all I could get was the dipper. Looked down into the crater and saw soft darkness. Made me want to go down and sit at the center and eat some Saltines, so I could say I've been there. Be good.

    love,
    Felice

I wondered where she got hot pink ink way out there. I cranked open my bedroom window and leaned against the screen, then I took out the screen altogether to let the night air in.

Chapter

Six

PEG'S ROOMMATE MABEL WAS A TINY, PINK-skinned woman with hair that fell to her shoulders in waves of gray and white. She was friends with both Ginny and Peg. Mabel could walk, but she had to take it slow. Peg and Ginny and Mabel would often sit in the hall together drinking coffee and gathering incidents for Peg's book about the nursing home.

"The aides are skipping baths again," Mabel might call out, shaking her head, and I'd have a voice besides my own conscience reminding me to bathe Mr. Pierson.

"Ummhmm, and did you hear Shelley screaming over dinner?" Ginny might say, leaning back in her wheel-chair. "You just have to spend a little time with her and she'll eat fine, but that damn girl was cramming food in her mouth like she was stuffing a turkey."

"I'll write it up tonight." Peg had sounded thick and strange to me until I stopped being so distracted by the strangeness that I couldn't hear the sense. She always made sense.

MABEL WENT INTO the hospital one week with the flu and came out talking about Billy. No one had ever heard of Billy before. He was on his way home, Mabel said. He'd be back any time now, and everybody had to leave room for Billy.

At first Peg and Ginny sat with Mabel in the hall as usual, Mabel talking about Billy, and Peg taking notes with a new urgency, writing down everything Mabel said and when she said it. But gradually Peg stopped listening and talking to Mabel at all. She took to drinking her coffee in the room they shared while Mabel was settled out in the hall.

Ginny still took coffee from the tray I brought around and would offer a cup to Mabel, who always said, "Oh yes, please," but then she'd sit there and let it get cold without taking a sip. She said she didn't like to start until Billy was there.

Peg couldn't stand it. I overheard her talking with Ginny about it one afternoon when I was in Peg's bathroom emptying her leg bag. I was rinsing it out and half listening to a talk show Peg had on about whether or not it was right for a woman to get a job and leave her young children at a day-care center. The experts were saying it would permanently harm a child when I heard a bang, followed by Ginny's voice, and knew that she had run her chair into the door on the way into the room.

Those minor collisions happened all the time, and Ginny didn't even stop to catch her breath. "Peg," she said, "we miss taking coffee with you."

Peg's answer was jerky and hard to understand. "We who? Maybe you miss me, but Mabel has no idea if I'm there or not."

Ginny sounded tired. "Mabel does know. She knows, and she doesn't like how you're treating her. Neither do I. The wandering isn't her fault."

Peg's voice started out low, but by the time she finished speaking, it was as near to shouting as she could come. "Whose fault is it, then? It's not like she had a stroke or something. She gave up on us and she's living in some reality of her own, where all that matters is that goddamn Billy."

I turned the water on in the bathroom to remind Peg that I was there.

Ginny knocked the coffee off the tray on her chair, startled by the sudden sound. "Shit! Who's that?" I came out with a washcloth to wipe the coffee up.

"Sorry," I said. "I didn't mean to listen."

Ginny broke her usual rule of being sweet to the aides. "Just leave that. We're talking."

Peg dropped her hand toward her leg. "Sorry, Ginny. She's got to put my leg bag back on."

I brought the bag in from the bathroom and tried my best imitation nurse smile. "This will just take a second."

Peg smiled back. "Take your time. Just don't get my leg hairs caught in the Velcro."

I laughed nervously and was careful with the strap. I had the feeling that Peg was stalling Ginny, who was wearing her red slippers that made me think of Dorothy in *The Wizard of Oz*. In another mood I might have asked her which way to the yellow brick road, but she was rubbing her cheek against her shoulder, messing up her makeup, so I knew she was upset.

I stood up. "Finished. I'll see you two later."

Peg gave me a soft "Bye." I shut the door on my way out, although I knew that would never last. The nurses liked the doors open so they could hear anything going on inside. I took Mabel's coffee from her tray as she sat in the hall. She said, "Is Billy home yet?"

GINNY AND PEG must have gotten something talked out, because Peg eased up on Mabel. The three of them drank their coffee together once in a while, but things were never really the same. Mabel spent most of her afternoons sitting in the courtyard or scrubbing the walls with a paper towel. The hardest times, though, were the nights when Mabel couldn't sleep, when she lay in bed and said, "Please, God, let me die," over and over. Peg was a light sleeper with few dreams. She had "let me die" soaking into her with her own growing tiredness.

I would hear it when I came in to check Mabel's bed and empty Peg's bag. Mabel would stop while I was moving about the room, but as I walked out the door, I could hear her start up again, "Please, God, let me die."

"Get me up," said Peg into the gray light as I passed her bed one bad night.

"I can't, Peg, I just don't have time." It was true. I had to hurry or I'd never get all of the beds checked before my break.

Peg seemed to swell under her sheets. "Get me out of this bed." So I let the bedrails down, and she sat in the common room watching TV.

I went to sit with her when I finally did take my break. Tom Snyder was on. Peg was looking through her notebook, turning the pages with her fists. I could have stuck my own fist in my mouth after I said it, but I came right out and asked her, "Peg, do you miss your fingers?"

She gave me the look of a woman who has had a hard night. The gaze of her wandering eye slid across my cheek. "Don't be stupid, they're right here."

I always found myself saying things to Peg I would usually keep to myself. I argued. "But you can't use them."

Peg wasn't arguing. She was slumping, bone tired, her feet slipped off the foot rests. I think she was too worn out to get annoyed. "Char, I used to think you paid attention. I use them."

I watched her stiff face, and plunged on. "But isn't there anything you miss?"

Peg's voice was even more quiet than usual. "There's a lot I miss. I miss going out easy, just slipping on my boots on impulse and stepping out the door. I miss walking out on fools. I miss being on time. I miss having money to burn and picking someone up on a three-day weekend with my folks out of town." She made a noise in her throat. "I'm a fireman's daughter. Did you know that? Have you noticed that picture on my bedside table? That's me and my dad, with his whole squad. One of the guys wanted to marry me, but I wasn't interested in taking anyone else on. Now there's Ginny and her beautiful shoes." I touched her arm. She looked at me sharp. "You know, an orderly got fired for making out with Hannah Schneider. Hannah told me she was kissing him back."

I felt embarrassed. "That's awful." I wished she hadn't told me that at this particular moment.

"Yeah, Hannah said it wasn't such a great kiss, but it was better than nothing." Peg looked back up at the screen. "Listen, I'm trying to watch a show here."

I stood up. "Yeah, I'm off soon. Good night."

Peg asked permission from the front office to set up her typewriter in the common room but was denied. It would be too disruptive for the other patients, Mr. Jonas felt. So Ginny, who was paying extra not to have a room-mate, let Peg set it up in her room, next to the unused bed. Peg had to listen to "Cupid" play over and over, but she said it helped her concentrate.

ONE NIGHT I worked the late shift, subbing for Kiley, who was at a wedding and had promised to smuggle out tastes of magnificence for me. The halls looked big and empty, shed of their afternoon caginess. I finished a round of bed checks and was going to join Peg and Ginny in the common room where they were watching TV. I heard silence from Mabel's bed as I passed, except for a low buzz that might have been a snore or a purr. I felt like a tired animal myself, padding home in my soft-soled shoes. All I wanted was a Pepsi and a semi-padded chair: a small break. Perez was lying down in a spare bed where Mrs. Merker had died a few days ago. She and Mrs. Merker had gotten along great. They used to sing reli-gious songs together as Perez put her to bed. Perez had given me a sample as she slid off her shoes and lay down, cracked heels showing through her nylon socks. "Ellen Merker wouldn't mind one bit."

It really was okay. I was awake, the beds had been checked, and everyone was either asleep or staring awake, as was their nightly habit. Iris's restraints were untangled and secure, which would last at least an hour.

The quietness suggested night, even though the lights were bright in the hall. I stopped in the door of the com-mon room. Peg had her stronger arm resting on the arm of Ginny's chair. Ginny's hands were both in her lap, but she was turned, as if to get a better look at the screen, so her shoulder, soft and bare in her sleeveless blouse, was touching Peg's, or so close to touching that I had to call it that in the wide, empty space of the common room. Dan the Furniture Man was screeching, "It's a sale!" Peg said something I couldn't catch, then Ed started in with "Nurse, nurse, nurse," and I turned back up the hall, although I knew he wouldn't be able to tell me what he wanted when I got to his bed.

I WROTE BACK to Felice, but it was hard. I could forget her at work, where I was surrounded by people who were different from anyone I had ever expected to meet, but anytime I was on my own, she would come floating up. Missing her was a background to everything I did, and it was uncomfortable to bring it enough to the front to write her.

> Dear Felice:
>
> How are you doing? Things are boring here without you. All I do is work. The nursing home's not too bad, although one girl who started the same time I did has another job at Dunkin' Donuts already. Said she'd rather smell sugar than shit. She was the one who walked around with the tape player blasting "Only the Good Die Young." Please. I just hope nobody really does die near me. I don't think about that much.
>
> It's all starting to seem normal, even Mabel, who's always scrubbing the walls with a Kleenex and waiting for a ghost named Billy. Her roommate is a much younger woman. Peg. I like her a lot. Other aides warned me about her, said she was picky, but she just knows what she wants. She organized a food protest that turned into a riot.

Peg has a friend named Ginny who plays the Temptations and Sam Cooke all day long. I leave the arm off the turntable, so the music keeps coming even if nobody shows up to change the record. She has beautiful shoes: black loafers, blue spike heels, violet pumps. Even her chair has red wheels. Her brother-in-law owns a shoe factory. I had expected everyone here to be at least half dead, so I am surprised at all this life.

Oh, Felice, I wish I could really talk to you. My dance moves are getting rusty, too. I need some practice with you. Hope the rocks are splitting open like sliced apples at your feet so that you can see their hearts. Write soon.

Love,

Char

I dug out some tinsel left over from Christmas and stuck it in the envelope to make the letter exciting. I could hear Mom in the kitchen, humming "Heard It Through the Grapevine" along with the radio. I wondered why I had written so much about Ginny when it was Peg I was getting close to, but I couldn't find any words to give Peg's slow-voiced stubborness and wandering eye to Felice. I licked the envelope and decided to keep most of Peg to myself.

EUGENIA CRIBBS WAS a substantial woman. She was shorter than me but weighed more. Every night she would wait in her usual pink, fuzzy slippers and flower-print cotton robe for an aide to put her to bed. The robe snapped up the front like almost all of Eugenia's clothes. Arthritis had ruined her fingers for buttons. The exception to her snaps-only policy was her long-line bra, which she needed an aide to unhook.

"Hi, honey," said Eugenia one night when I arrived. She tilted her head so she could look at me through the magnifying part of her bifocals. "Running late tonight?"

Eugenia was one of the alert patients. "Sorry to keep you waiting," I said briskly. "We're short-staffed." Her eyes looked big as superballs as I peered back at her through the wrong side of her lenses.

"Well, let's get at it." Eugenia started unsnapping her robe and telling me things, reminding me to hang three washcloths on her bedrail and to leave a pair of clean underwear folded under her pillow and her eyeglasses case where she could reach it. Eugenia was fussy. She kept a basket full of rhinestone necklaces, jewelled lipstick cases, and big satin-covered earrings on her bedside table, next to a sign that said DO NOT TOUCH, but I reached in and rattled them with my fingers when she wasn't looking, and they threw off colored glints of light.

Eugenia stood up for a moment so that I could slip off her robe, then sat back down and leaned forward so I could unhook her bra. It was a formidable garment, with underwired cups and many hooks. It was shiny white against her flour-white skin. Eugenia groaned as I worked. I opened the hooks, releasing the light smell of sweat and powder. Her back spread and bloomed into unexpected freckles and red fold-lines exposed after being pressed against themselves all day. I slipped into a rhythm working the hooks that made me remember how Mom used to call me into her bedroom to fasten her into *her* long-line bra. When she went any place fancy, she felt the need of extra support. It was the same rhythm of tug and hook, only in reverse, until Mom was packed in for the night. Then she'd put on her shimmering slip, soft-draped yellow dress, and textured green high heels. She had been erect and breathless.

Now I moved around in front of Eugenia to slip the straps off her shoulders. I leaned down to pull the big-necked nightgown over her head. When I stepped back, she looked up at me and said, "Sugar, you've got on the wrong kind of bra."

"What?" I folded my arms across my chest.

Eugenia pointed her magnifying lenses straight at my breasts. "No use trying to hide. You're spilling out of the cups."

I couldn't believe she'd been looking at my underwear while I'd been dreaming over hers. I unfolded my arms to tug on a shoulder strap, blushing. Eugenia pushed her glasses higher up on her nose. "It's a fact of life. Some people have humps on their backs. You and I have big boobs." I didn't want to, but I looked down at her breasts, so large and obvious now that they were loose under her nightgown. Eugenia pointed to redirect my attention to the garment I had just hung over the rail of the bed to air out. "That's very good for figure control," she said.

I looked at her fat, powdered face with her giant eyes and white hair falling in waves around her cheeks. She gazed back at me with an expression of interest and goodwill so intense that I had to look away. I tugged on my bra strap through my tunic again. I couldn't think of anything to say.

Eugenia stood without my help and seated herself on the bed. Her nightgown fell around her in filmy folds. "It's worth it," she said, "to keep up a good front."

She reached out and gave my belly a tweak with a very small smile on her face.

I WENT BACK to the mountains by myself. I brought a six-pack to drink but ended up leaving it on the floor of the back seat, untouched. The Pinto dragged itself around the curves. I sang out the open window, "And I've had so many men before in very many ways. He's just one more." I was feeling melancholy and experienced. It was Thursday, my day off, so there was no one else parked next to the picnic tables. I had on the cheap rubber thongs I was wearing everywhere I didn't have to wear white that summer. I stubbed my toe the moment I stepped out of the car. My big toenail tore. "Gneiss," I said, looking at the nondescript rock. At least it hadn't been a piece of glass from the shattered bottle near the Pinto's rear tire. I thought about what it would take to get Peg out here. Not much, really, just widening the path and getting rid of the really big rocks. Her chair could handle the rest, as long as the grade wasn't too steep.

Someone would have to drive her up, though, and I danced away from that, skipping up the trail. It felt good to move fast just then.

Chapter Seven

IRIS, THE BREAD WOMAN, LOOKED DANGEROUS. Her nose was gone, eaten down to raw holes by some disease. I never tried to find out what. Her fingers were thin and strong. She would grab at my clothes when I came in to change the beds. She was always restrained, tied to the bed so she couldn't reach me, but her reputation for meanness meant that her sheets weren't changed quite every day. To change them while she was in bed, I had to roll her on one side, bunch the dirty sheets close to her back, spread out the clean ones, then roll her over the hump onto her other side. Most patients were as light and easy to roll as dry logs. Some even helped. Iris fought.

I almost always did change her bed, though. I would touch her lightly, asking where it hurt the least, and watch her skin tear anyway under my hands. One day she was quiet, so I leaned down and stroked her cheek.

Right away I was afraid I would catch something. What had eaten her nose away? She opened her eyelids. They were transparent. I didn't think they kept out much light. She looked up and said, "Cancer." She could have meant me and my white uniform pantsuit.

If Iris was up in her chair, she had to be tied to the railing, or she'd be hitting people in the hall. Even tied to the rail, she'd make a swipe at someone and end up hanging there, dangling by her restraints. On the Fourth of July, the nurse told me to put some underwear on Iris. Important people were coming to visit her. They hadn't come by the end of my shift, but the nurse had heard that Iris used to be a big Washington lawyer.

That night when I went home, I got out the ladder and climbed up on the low roof of our house to watch the fireworks. The air was cool on my bare legs, and I sat with my arms crossed over my knees. There were a few faint wheels of light in the sky toward the mountains, but I mostly just listened to the toy noises of the sparklers, fountains, and cherry bombs going off all over the neighborhood. I remembered Felice and me as little girls on the fifth of July, going to all the gutters and yards, picking up burnt-out bottle rockets. We had been sure we could use them for something good, if we just found enough of them. When we had two grocery sacks full, we glued them on cardboard in a great sunburst circle, little cylinders of powder and burnt fuses facing in, stick stems out. It was a great sign for a clubhouse, so we made up a club to go with it. The initiation ceremony was letting layer after layer of glue dry on our palms until we could stick a needle in and not feel a thing. Felice told me about blood brothers, how they cut themselves and mixed their blood, but we decided that we would do the opposite: we would stick ourselves and not bleed.

Blood brought Iris to mind. I rubbed my bare toes on the tar shingles of the roof. I hadn't known that anyone could be down to such a fragile layer of skin and clamoring bones and still keep such strength in her. Not many of the patients had the energy for fury. I imagined Iris in a plush hat and a sharp suit with padded shoulders, stepping briskly up a stretch of white marble steps in the official Washington sun. There would be clusters of men in dark business clothes climbing, too, but they couldn't keep up with Iris. Even then her bones carved a place for her face in the air. She didn't recognize dream time—she read the rules of government late into the night. She didn't need memory. She had reference books. She had red fingernails. Newspaper reporters had called them talons. One of the men in dark clothes was at her heels. His white cuffs and collar caught the brightness of the sun. Even in black strap heels, her thin legs carried her so precisely that her straight skirt didn't stir. She had papers, important papers, in a leather case.

She reached the top of the steps. The man with the white cuffs bounded up after her. She turned and looked out over the city. He breathed hard and took out a beautiful crisp handkerchief to wipe his brow.

"I don't care much for this case," she said, leaning into the view.

"It's not our business to care for them." He was bluffing toughness. "It's our business to win them."

The other men were striding by them now, nodding hello, calling her name, patting his back, stepping over the threshold through the big double doors. A woman passed, smelling of lilac. A client, thought Iris. She could tell by the wide eyes.

The woman turned back at the threshold and looked directly at Iris. Her cheeks were flushed with the exertion of the climb. Her wide eyes were black.

"My dear," she said from the doorway, "how do you breathe up here?"

Iris felt triumphant. She knows I belong, she thought. Her reply was cordial. "It's like flying. Just something you get used to."

The client fingered her ring. "I like being earthbound myself."

The strain of being ignored stretched the man's voice when he spoke. "Iris isn't afraid of planes. She's not afraid of anything."

The two women lifted eyebrows at each other. "He's wrong, of course," said the client.

"Of course," answered Iris as she moved toward the door.

I WATCHED A high one flare three colors into the sky. It took a long time to fade, and others went off while its smoke was still hanging in the air. I shivered. I was playing with Iris's life, as if she had to have an old sin of too much pride or too much success to make her earn her present furious pain. What did I know about it? Maybe her uncle just reached for her face too many times, crying, "Got your nose!" sticking his own thumb out of his fist and wiggling it at her until she got the metaphor. His thumb was her nose. Her skinny body was my job. What else could it be? I climbed down the ladder and went into the house.

The next day at work, Iris called me from her room, "Come here, sweetheart." When I came, she grabbed the chain around my neck where the keys to the wing hung. She twisted the chain and pulled. I struggled with her a minute before jerking it loose. Nothing hurt. Iris just shrank back against the pillow. I wore my keys inside my shirt after that.

I DREAMED FELICE all summer. It seemed odd that no one saw her but me. Even Mom, who noticed from fifty paces if I spilled a drop of juice on my blouse, didn't catch a glimpse. But I found myself clearing off the passenger seat for Felice every time I got into the Pinto. I'd sit at the long traffic lights on my way to work, playing her name over and over in my head, working up a nice haze of distraction. I'd see her flat like a photo, leaning over me the night she braided my hair, then I'd push the picture, trying to give it a shape that would pass for life. She'd blanch and fade, and I'd find myself making a left turn into the nursing home parking lot. The daydream got me there, got me a lot of places that summer.

I tried to keep Felice real by saying her name. I told people I was missing her, but "missing my friend," even "missing my best friend," sounded too hollow and light. Mom just looked at me over the mixing bowl and nodded. Mr. Pierson didn't even nod, of course.

Things were slow on the wing one day. It was after lunch, long before supper, and I had almost finished the beds. Perez was doing baths. Eugenia and Ed and Shelley were drowsing in their chairs, heads dropping to their chests, faces soft. Mabel was washing the wall with a brown paper towel, and it was as if she drew all of the energy in the wing into the dry circles she was rubbing on the plaster. It was very hot. I pushed my cart into Ginny's room. Martha and the Vandellas were spinning on the record player, but only Peg was there, bent over the pad on her lap, writing. She wore a red cotton shirt, and it was a long time before she looked up.

"Where's Ginny?" I asked, getting busy with the sheets. I was always a little edgy alone with Peg, which confused me, since I liked her a lot. Maybe it was the way one of her eyes had a way of separating its gaze from the other and wandering to odd angles of the room. Now it glanced off my hip while the rest of Peg looked me in the face.

"She's in the hospital for tests," Peg said with a tough little jerk of her shoulders. She looked sad. I made tight corners with the blanket and watched Peg take a sip of coffee. She drank through a crazy straw someone had given her, clear plastic that did loop-d-loops before it got from the cup to her mouth.

Peg noticed my glance. "Watching coffee take those loops always makes me think of blood vessels and intestines," she said, pulling away from the straw.

I watched the coffee, thinking it looked a bit grisly as it drained back into her cup. "I can see it."

Peg took another sip. I put the dirty sheets in the hamper. "Ginny's been in a lot of pain," said Peg.

I sat down on the bed I had just made. "Mmmm. I'm sorry."

"You get used to a certain amount of it—" she thrust her shoulders against the air again—"but it wears you out."

"Some mountains form by thrust." I was changing the subject. I'd been mooning over one of Felice's letters on break, and geology was on my mind. "Others form by erosion or block faulting."

Peg knocked the straw away from her face with her chin. "Really?"

"I've got this friend named Felice," I said, swinging my feet. "She likes rocks."

"Yeah?" Peg swung to look at me with her abrupt, wall-eyed sharpness.

I picked up a fingernail clipper from her bedside table. "You want me to do this for you? I've got time."

"Okay."

72

I took Peg's hand and rested it on my lap. Her fingers were folded against her palm, but I could get to the nails. Her skin was red and soft. I began to clip.

"Felice, my friend Felice," I said, "is gone for the summer." I noticed a spattering of freckles on Peg's inner wrist. "I miss her a lot."

Peg made a noise like the one I'd just made. "Mmmm. I hate it when Ginny is gone for even a day." Her nails were falling in white wisps onto the blanket. I brushed them together in a little pile.

"I hope Ginny is all right." Ginny's name carried echoes of Felice when I said it. I concentrated on cutting an even curve on Peg's index finger: no sharp edges, not too close to the quick.

"I don't like missing her," said Peg. I felt myself nod. "It's too complicated. I keep things simple, and she's got these frilly curtains."

I kept listening to the sharp click of the clippers. I heard a crackle in Peg's voice, like the sound cellophane makes when it's pulled off a package. She was about to unwrap something for me. I held the warm weight of her hand lightly.

"Shiny shoes," said Peg, "doo-wop music, bladder spasms, five sisters, an ex-husband. The works."

I checked for smoothness with my thumb. I wanted to tell Peg something private about Felice, to hear if our overlapping voices sounded as important as just Peg's did, but I couldn't think of what to say.

"Felice's mother hurts her." As soon as I said it, I knew that I'd gone too far. I started working on Peg's other hand.

Peg did something with her eyebrows. "That's a crying shame."

I felt queasy. Felice wouldn't like me talking about her family behind her back, and I had missed the heart of what I wanted Peg to know about Felice.

This hand was as warm and still as the other, and I had a sudden uncomfortable urge to press it against my thigh, to try to get a message out that way. I shook the feeling off and opened my mouth. Another Felice quotation came out. "There are rocks at the bottom of the Grand Canyon over a billion years old."

Peg's wandering eye circled up a beam of light from the window. She gave one of her shrugs. "Is this some kind of code?"

I finished Peg's hand and placed it back on the arm of the chair. I noticed sweat dripping down her forehead and reached into the pocket of my tunic for a clean washrag. I got up off the bed and leaned over to wipe her face. I had moved closer, but I felt safer, as if we were settling back into place. I answered her. "It's geology."

Peg took a sip of cold coffee through her straw. I glanced into the hall and saw Ginny being pushed past the door, looking tired and drawn.

"I'll take her," I called to the pimply boy clenching the handgrips.

"How are you?" I asked Ginny, on duty.

"Hospitals kill me," she said. I nodded, wheeled her in next to Peg, and left. I didn't look back to see if they rubbed arms or not.

Chapter Eight

PEOPLE GOT TENSE BEFORE MEALS AT THE nursing home, especially when it was too hot to eat. One night the pressure felt higher than usual as I wheeled the cartful of trays in from the kitchen. It was like the feeling I got sitting down to supper at home without having brushed my hair, waiting for Dad to let me have it. Except at this job, I was Dad, or at least Mom, trying to shove spoons into a few mouths and keep a lid on the family pot.

Perez was going from room to room feeding the slow people and setting up trays for those like Ginny, who could make it clear when they didn't feel like eating with the group. I had everybody else gathered at one end of the dining hall. I started passing out trays, cutting food, and opening cartons of milk. I had to keep pushing my hair back out of my eyes. Mr. Pierson was sitting stock-still, staring over his plate at the wall. Mabel sat beside him, cutting up her meat and slipping it into the carton she held between her legs. She saved her meals for Billy. Whenever I caught her eye, she'd take a bite herself. She gave Mr. Pierson's hand a pat every now and then. "There," she'd say. When she finished emptying her plate, she started on his.

All of us could hear Iris cussing at Perez down the hall. Ed and Judith and Violet were waiting for their dinners, seated at the table, making comments about Shelley's appetite and Iris's language. Everyone was sweating. My bangs were sticking to my forehead, and my eyes stung. I made a quick circuit to take the foil off of everyone's juice. I offered a spoonful of corn to Shelley, which she swallowed, giving me a crooked-tooth grin. She took another bite, in a good mood. I rescued a bit of Mr. Pierson's dinner and offered it to him. He opened his mouth and shut it with the meat on his tongue.

I gave his shoulder a squeeze. My palm left a damp spot on the cloth. "Come on, Mr. Pierson, chew a little."

Mabel leaned forward. "Oh, please do. Please chew."

I tapped her plate with my finger. "Right, Mabel. Don't you think you should eat a little more of your own dinner?"

She rearranged her skirt so that it covered the carton. "No, thank you. I'm waiting for Billy." I could see her blood moving up closer to her skin. She was so thin. I started to insist, but Eugenia needed help cutting her meat, and so did Peg. Their food was getting cold while we all sweated.

"Nurse! Nurse!" Eugenia was tired of waiting. Shelley threw her spoon. Mabel was trying to get Mr. Pierson to drink so she could have the carton. Milk dribbled down the outside of his mouth, but he swallowed as he tipped it to his lips. I picked up the spoon, gave Shelley another bite of corn, then started slicing for Eugenia.

Eugenia got a look of fierce concentration on her face as she picked up her fork. The liver spots on her hands trembled and danced. "Very slow service around here," she whispered loudly to Ed. He swallowed, nodded, and dipped up another heap of applesauce.

I felt slow, slow and hot and responsible for too many lives. I gave Shelley a spoonful of gravy and dropped half of it onto her bib. I was rushing her. The front of Mr. Pierson's shirt was soaked with milk. Shelley was getting cranky because I kept forgetting to give her time to swallow. "Here, Shelley, have some more. Open up, sweetie. That's good, that's a good girl." Shelley was maybe nineteen, a couple of years older than me, but she was so bent and soft and guileless, she seemed like a baby.

I cut the meat smaller, gave her another bite, then moved Peg's straw. "Is that all right? Good?"

There were no windows. My polyester uniform held the sweat, kept it next to me, as I fed. Eugenia's fork did the polka to her face. Shelley shook her walker. I mopped up Mr. Pierson, sweating and trying not to be too present.

Peg leaned forward to speak, faint and slow. "Char," she said. I had to stop to listen. "Mary had a little lamb."

"What?" I stepped closer.

"The doctor fainted." She sat back in her chair, pleased with her joke.

I stood there holding a milk-soaked bib, dripping sweat, trying to understand, but when I finally got it, I laughed and Peg laughed and Shelley beat her spoon on her tray. I propped open the fire door to let a breeze in while we finished the meal.

MOM WAS COOKING when I got up the next morning. She was making yogurt and cottage cheese diet salad, listening to a talk show on the radio. The guest was a woman who had written a book about single men, their hobbies, and their fears. The host said, "Tell the truth. This is for girls who want to pick up guys, right?"

The guest laughed. "Are you single?"

Mom switched over to the jazz station. "Good morning," she said. "Did you lose any weight this morning?"

I leaned on the refrigerator door, deciding whether I wanted breakfast or lunch. "Yep. Half a pound."

Mom was squeezing lemon juice into the low-cal yogurt. "Oh, honey, that's great." She sprinkled some Bacos into the salad, and some into her hand to feed to the dog.

"Here, Ralphie, that'll look better on you than it would on me." She mixed the cottage cheese in with the yogurt and offered me a bite.

"Your cheeks really do look thinner. You can have this for lunch, if you like."

"Okay," I said, taking a bottle of catsup from the refrigerator. "How'd you do?"

Mom put plastic wrap over the rest of the salad and sat down at the table with a celery stick. "Not as well as you did. I didn't gain, but I didn't lose anything, either."

I was introducing cottage cheese-Baco-yogurt to a pool of catsup. "At least you held steady."

Mom sighed, leaning on her elbows. "I know. It's just discouraging."

I knew how she felt. I had lost half a pound by standing on the scale and leaning on the sink until the pointer stopped where I wanted it to be, then gradually returning my weight to my feet until it stopped someplace better than yesterday, but possible. All in preparation for the first question of every morning.

Mom reached for her meal chart and her recipe book to write down what she had eaten yesterday and to plan what we would all eat next week. A wisp of celery floated from the corner of her mouth and landed smack in the middle of the piece of extra material that she had sewn into her dress to cover the cleft between her breasts. It worked with her bra to create a shelf effect.

She brushed the celery off with a little flourish of her hand, then said, "Ahem," nodding toward my own chest. I had dribbled catsup on my t-shirt. As usual, crumbs that ended up on other people's laps landed on my breasts. Family heritage.

"Oops." I walked over to the sink and dabbed at my shirt with a sponge. "Maybe I need a bib, like some of the folks at work."

"Try a little dish soap," said Mom. "How is work?"

I held my t-shirt away from my skin and shook it back and forth, hoping it would dry. "It wears me out. They need to hire more aides."

Mom was rereading her recipe for Cheesy Hamburger Pie. "Hmm. Maybe we could have this for supper with Lite cheese and no crust. You be sweet to those patients, Charlotte. Think of Gram."

I thought of my grandmother. She loved to put on her magnifying glasses that made her eyes look the size of giant jawbreakers, get in her Buick, and drive the wide, long roads with the cruise control set for eighty-five miles per hour. She would go out to the Ladybird Mall to do a little shopping. "Gram told me once she'd take the shotgun she uses on skunks and put it in her mouth if anyone mentioned a home to her."

Mom wrote "Instant Breakfast" on her shopping list. "That won't be necessary if she keeps driving like she does."

Sometimes Mom surprised me and got tough. It made me wonder about her childhood with Gram and Daddy Frank, who had died when I was seven. All his name suggested to me was thick fingers and jars of grass with fireflies. As I put my plate into the dishwasher, it struck me that Mom wasn't born to the suburbs, not like me. I'd seen pictures of Mom, young, on a horse, with those family breasts pushing out fringe on a fancy cowgirl shirt, and the family thighs spreading wide and strong against the shining brown saddle. Mom wasn't born to the suburbs, but she had studied home economics, underlining the parts about the four basic food groups and family life. I had found some of her old textbooks on the top shelf behind a stack of Reader's Digest Condensed Classics. One passage marked in blue ink noted that in marriage physical love was important, but it wasn't everything.

Mom had married my daddy, had Jeff and me, and taken on Moody as if it fit her like her favorite girdle. She did mention the tight spaces between the houses, but she took the dog to the park a lot, where she found wild asparagus, and once she saw a fox.

I wanted to ask her what she would really do if Gram got sick, but it didn't seem like a question with an answer. Bring her here to Moody if she could travel this far, I guessed. I didn't like to think of Gram here with just a driveway to park in and no place she wanted to go.

I remembered myself as a nine-year-old in a stretched turtle top, walking into the kitchen to ask Mom why she and Daddy had picked this place to live in. I had been reading Jack London and dreaming of the Yukon. She had handed me the cheese grater. She was peeling potatoes into the sink in her slow, thorough way. A big pot of water was boiling on the stove behind her, and she was defrosting a hunk of ground meat on another burner, stopping now and then to scrape the gray softened meat off the frozen core. She had a toothpick in her mouth to keep her from tasting while she cooked. She took it out to speak.

"We didn't think about it that much, honey," she said, tugging my shirt down where it kept riding up over my tight young belly. "Moody had good schools, this house had a window over the sink for me, and it wasn't on the edge of any trouble, like that integration we got into in Oklahoma. We could afford to live here, and it seemed like a good place for you to grow up."

Mom started to tuck the tag back into the neck of my shirt, but I squirmed away. "But integration is good," I said. I had had a day off from school when Martin Luther King Jr. was killed.

Mom put her toothpick back in her mouth. "Mmm," she said. She started pushing peels into the garbage disposal. "Charlotte, I was raised thinking it was my duty to be nice to black people. It wasn't until we lived in Oklahoma that it occurred to me that some of them might not care to be nice back." Mom glanced out the window into our yard. "The grass needs cutting." She flipped on the disposal. It growled. "It's best to stay out of all that."

I was getting down to the nub of the cheese, grating the tips of my fingers a bit.

"Careful, Char. That's enough cheese." Mom scooped it onto a paper towel and put it on the kitchen scale to weigh it. "Three ounces. That's plenty for you and me. Did you lose any weight today?"

"Yes, a pound." I was a cool liar, even then.

Mom smiled around her toothpick. "Good girl. Every little bit helps."

I KEPT NOTICING the motion of time that summer. It was the opposite of the motion of rocks, which seemed to sit solidly in one place but were really always shifting. Most of the people at the nursing home seemed to trip in and out of time past, dream time, meal time. A few, like Peg, chose the austerities of the present. Someone like Mr. Pierson, though, seemed to have passed out of the motion of time altogether to join the slow dance of the rocks.

Mr. Pierson kept silence. He didn't even speak with his eyes or his soft pink skin or his bones. He slept with his knees approaching his chin, curled up like something younger than a child. I asked Perez why no one used his first name, which was Joseph, and she handed me a pile of clean sheets, still warm from the laundry cart. "He's a mannerly man," she said. "He always had a fine bearing." Perez spoke politely to Mr. Pierson during the course of her work and had been known to favor him with a hymn in the shower room, so I knew she held him in high regard.

So did I, although I couldn't say why. He was almost shiny—not in the way Ginny was shiny, with fine sweaters and a wide-awake light—but in a soft way, like a lump of gypsum. He reminded me of different things, depending on whether I was pushing him or lifting him or giving him a glance as I rushed past in the hall. He was another like Iris, who somehow suggested his own history to me, as Iris had, without offering evidence of being anything except fully absorbed in his tucked-up quiet.

He had very little hair, which we combed sideways. His scalp was quietly flaking away, as was the skin on his shoulders and arms. He would open his lips to accept food if I held a spoon to his mouth, but he ate mechanically, as if he were having a thought that could not be interrupted because it was so strong.

I looked at him with interest, partly because I could. I could stare at him as long as I wanted, and he wouldn't look away or tell me I was rude. He wouldn't curse me like Iris, or stare me down like Peg. He would just keep sitting bent and still.

I had a dream of Mr. Pierson as a gardener, tapping tiny seeds from a white pack. Everything was in close-up, as if I were a camera left filming on the ground. They were celery seeds, and they fell more lightly than pepper from a mill. He blew down to cover them with a puff of earth. His knuckles were big, and one finger had a pale stripe, as if he usually wore a ring, but it was gone. In my dream, I knew he'd lost it in the garden. His sleeves were rolled up, and his forearms were veiny and hairy and brown from the sun. His hands were so big, I could see the white half-moons on his fingernails, one thumb gone black from a bruise. Then I heard the shovel in the dirt, saw the red-brown curve of it as he loosened the soil. I saw his muddy boot press the shovel. I panned up and pulled back until he went from being a giant hand and a giant shoe to a weathered man standing among the beds, with seedlings coming up unnaturally fast. Bib lettuce sprouted, red lettuce, slim onions, tiny celery spikes, fuzzy-stemmed tomatoes, broccoli looking the same as collards in the first leafing, then reaching up with their specific true leaves, all growing in fast slow motion, like a Disney nature short, while Mr. Pierson pulled out his shovel and stuck it in a bucket of clean sand. He pulled a parsnip that had wintered over out of the dirt, swung it over his head and threw it—hard as David threw the rock at Goliath in the Bible—square into the heart of the garden. The plants parted to let it land, and the dirt around the parsnip started whirling and flaking into the air. Mr. Pierson coughed into the yellow bandana he pulled from the pocket of his overalls. The seedlings stopped growing before any had fruited, about shin high, green and thick. The whirling dust became rain. The plants were drinking, and Mr. Pierson bent his head back to the sky. The wind blew off his cap. I wasn't a camera, but a root, and I drank.

I got out of bed to get some tap water from the bathroom. The dog was grinding his teeth on the threshold of my bedroom door. As I curled under the sheet again, hot and half awake, the dream changed. Mr. Pierson was driving his old truck down the road with his dog. He stopped, got out, and began walking and singing at the top of his lungs. The dog ran ahead, then pulled up short, looking back as if to call him. Mr. Pierson changed the words of his song, singing, "Yes, my burry furred friend, I'll be with you in the end." The dog jumped up, as high as the man's arm, knowing better than to put his muddy feet on the overalls. The tree frogs sang, too, after the man and the dog had passed. Mr. Pierson picked up a rock. Pumice. He thought of his daughter, the scientist, in Iceland standing on the still warm ash of a ten-year-old field of volcanic rock.

I rolled over and wadded up my pillow under my cheek. I wasn't convinced by the pumice or the scientist, so I pushed myself into an emptier sleep.

The next evening I wheeled Mr. Pierson into his room. I didn't flick the switch because there was enough glare from the hall light. The other bed was empty; his roommate was in the hospital. There was nothing on Mr. Pierson's nightstand but his false teeth in their case. The morning aide hadn't bothered with them when she had gotten him up. I lifted him to his feet, and we pivoted. Then I lowered him so that he was sitting on the edge of the bed. He was light. I kept a hand on his shoulder to steady him as I pulled his nightshirt out from where it lay folded under his pillow. I took off his shirt, tugged off his pants, then slipped his nightshirt over his shoulders. The skin over his collarbone flaked a little under my fingers. I reached under his thighs and swung his legs up onto the mattress. He curled his knees up to his chin in a slow/fast motion like the seedlings in my dream. I pulled up the bedrail and stood looking at him. I had just put a man to bed.

Of course, I had put men and women to bed every night since I'd gotten this job. Before that, I'd been putting little boys and little girls to bed in a long chain of babysitting jobs from the time I was eleven. By now, it should have been as familiar as pulling weeds or making French toast, but in this temporarily private room with the light from the hall casting shadows on the floor tiles, I was suddenly shocked with my power. I reached down and tucked the sheet in around his neck. He didn't stir. A vein made a ridge in his forehead. "I'm just seventeen," I thought. "How come they trust me with this?"

I bent down full of experimentation and tenderness to gather Mr. Pierson into my arms and give him a kiss full on the mouth.

He pressed his lips to mine and put his arms around me. They felt strong. He said something that was almost a word in my ear.

I stood there holding him, moved. Then I let him down on the pillow, and his eyes slipped shut. It wasn't until I got off work that night and was driving home through the black, wet streets that I felt guilt. I knew my kiss was not for who he actually was. His hug had nothing to do with me, since he'd never even looked me in the face, but I hoped it was okay, this once, to short-cut like that to warmth.

I stayed gentle with Mr. Pierson within professional limits after that. He stayed silent, curled in his one deep thought.

Chapter

Nine

I HELPED MABEL OFF WITH HER HOUSEDRESS and onto the shower chair. She sat elegantly and waved her hand at me, as if she had just been ushered to the best seat in a very fine house. "Thank you, dear. You may go now."

"Sorry, Mabel, I've got to stick around for this." I turned on the nozzle, directing the water at the floor for a moment. "You tell me if it's too cold," I said, pointing the hose at her legs.

She sighed. "Puffballs are out today."

I soaped her and rinsed her while she talked about Billy on the farm, the chickens in the yard, and the greening woods. I half listened, the rest of me absorbed in furtive fascination with her body. The skin of her hips settled and spread over the shower seat. She had a light, shiny scar on her belly. I lifted the patient weight of one breast to wash under it. Her veins showed blue through her skin. She was talking garden now: the last battered collards and brussel sprouts that had clung on through the winter, the new early peas, mulching the asparagus with hay and getting dirty up to her elbows in black soil and dug-in vetch.

I was working lather into the kinked gray hairs under her arms, thinking I should offer to let her hold the soap and make herself as clean as she wanted, but I had so many beds to change before dinner that I didn't even try. Instead, I reached for the scant towel to start drying her off.

I had to keep tugging on the back of my tunic, which was riding up as I bent over Mabel. The folds of my back were slippery with steam and sweat. A familiar fact hit me as strange: bodies are secret. Once on vacation I'd seen little girls running with their shirts off in a hot Texas park, but Mom said no when I wanted to jump through the sprinklers, too. I'd seen pictures in a house where I used to babysit, in a magazine, stuck in a basket next to the toilet. The women were slick as rubber, one shade, and smooth all over. Their sanded cantaloupe breasts had hard nipples that stuck out like the knotted ends of balloons in silhouette. Everything else about their bodies was as stretched and hard as the chests and bellies of the boys in summer who took off their shirts to play kickball in the street. Hard as Ted from down the street, who would stop in on a night game of hide-and-seek to take Felice to the little shed out back. Sometimes Felice would come out kicking and threatening Ted with a kerosene can. Other times she'd come out held tight, tight under his arm. He would squeeze her shoulder, then put both arms around her and lift her into the air. I was too fat to be lifted, never thought of trying to lift her myself, but now I held out clean underpants for Mabel to step into, then raised her with one arm firm under her shoulder, tugging the waistband up around her waist. I pulled her housedress back on over her head, and fastened it up to where her member-of-society neckline tan was outlined in dark moles and rimmed with purplish white. I took her by the arm, and we walked down the hall with Mabel still talking country, talking Billy walking out to the marsh to look for fiddleheads way too early in the spring.

I HAD THE next day off. It was Saturday, Dad put his country-and-western 78s on the hi-fi, and we all did chores while they dropped. Jeff worked in the yard. I cleaned the bathroom to Tennessee Ernie Ford and Kay Starr, who had the feed-'em-in the-morning, change-'em, feed-'em-in-the-evening blues. I could hear my father in the kitchen slamming the cupboard doors because he couldn't find the bowl he wanted to make pancakes in, and Mom being sorry for being such a mess.

The front bathroom was pink. It had double sinks and triple medicine cabinets that were half full of aspirin and Band-Aids, rubbing alcohol and Jeff's new razors. I took Windex to the mirrored doors to wipe out the white flecks of toothpaste and soapy water. I cleaned the counters with Dow Bathroom Cleanser. I felt lavish smearing all that foam over the smooth sinks and smothering the faint grit in the shower stall. I was also uneasy, something to do with Dow and Vietnam. I wasn't sure what the connection was, but I thought I might have heard that there was one. I was relieved to go on to the Johnny Mop.

I dipped the blue scrubber into the toilet and thought about Mabel carrying water. I could see her as a dirty-necked girl in a loose smock, already with sloping shoulders and long skinny arms, hauling water from the well every day. The bucket handles cut into her palms, but there was no fudging, because there had to be water for drinking and cooking and washing up and keeping the garden alive in the heat. Mabel picked flowers on the way to the well, but all her strength had to go to the water on the way back to the kitchen. If she tripped over a root in the path, she had scraped knees and the walk back to the well. The water in the well looked mysterious, not trickling clear like in a stream, more like standing water in a ditch where frogs laid their jelly bowls full of eggs.

Mabel would sit on the edge of the well, dangling her legs inside against the moss, knowing her mama was waiting to hand her the rake.

I finished up by emptying the pink wastebasket and shaking out the throw rugs, hearing Ray Charles hit the words hard, doing "Crying Time."

I opened the sliding glass door and went out back to lean on the toolshed and read Felice's letter again.

> Dear Char:
>
> Been smoking up back here by the dumpster on my breaks, but Tony, the guy with the pot, didn't come in today. I hope he's not quitting. He took me to White Sands. I bought some swan sunglasses at the gas station on the drive down. I'll send you a snapshot. The sand really blazed. It was too hot to stand on, but we could run down the dunes. The only other cars on the road were army jeeps—guess they test rockets out there. Wild to be in a place that's piles and piles of just one thing. It's mostly crushed gypsum, with a little quartz mixed in. Guess that's

what a beach must be like, only with water, too. Next stop California (I wish). There was a strange little lake where nothing lives, except white beetles.

The job's okay. Tony's sweet. Mickey and Kenny and Rick are annoying, but we're getting along. Hope you're all right. Be good.

love,

Felice

I got the clippers from the toolshed and started trimming the tall grass along the fence, mad that Felice was picking up boy trash again. I could see her in the desert, drinking up the white sand with her skin. I could see her at the Mobil station, posing in front of the red-winged horse on the sign, squinting through her plastic sunglasses and waiting for him to click, or maybe she got the attendant to take a picture of them both; maybe he bought himself a pair with little pistols on the corners where hers had swans. How was she ever going to learn anything about landforms with some dumb pothead hanging around, leeching her time? I hit chainlink with the clippers and had to pull out a tough length of grass by hand. It wasn't that I didn't want her to have a life. It was just that her trip to White Sands had to be an overnight, and I suspected that she wasn't being consistent with her position on casual sex. We'd discussed it in depth. I'd said I thought it was fine, healthy even, to have fun whenever you could. Felice hadn't been so sure. She'd said she didn't want to waste any time. I'd maintained that as long as you enjoyed it, nothing could be a waste of time, but why the hell was Felice throwing herself after this Tony when she could be applying herself, testing the ash content of the soil, even digging for goddamn gold.

Felice had sent me gypsum dust in a little string pouch stuck into the bottom of the envelope with the letter. It was strange and shiny, a very fine, soft sand. Gypsum is low on the hardness chart. I sprinkled a pinch of it around my neck, for magic, then felt gritty. When I finished clipping the fenceline, I went in to take a shower.

The chrome was still gleaming, and there was that sharp chemical smell that I'd grown up with as clean, but Jeff had been in to wash his hands, so there were dirty suds lingering in the sink. I ran the water to send them on down the drain. Daddy's records were still spinning: "One Mint Julep" sounded jazzy and scratched.

I stepped into the shower stall and shut the clear glass door. The water spilled over me. My skin drank it in for one full minute. Then, because it was summer and water was rationed, I turned off both faucets at once. I was bare and damp. I reached for the soap. It was a new bar, big. I turned it in my palms, working up suds. I spread them down one side of my body and up the other, until my legs, my breasts, the folds of my sides, and the trough of my back were all coated with white. Everything felt loose and soft under my hands, except for my tough feet. I turned the water on again and leaned back so the soap didn't wash into my eyes. When I had rinsed clean, I stood in the shower another minute, just letting the water run to waste.

I turned to the corner of the stall and made a small cave. The walls of the cave were my body and the pink tile. The water was outside, beating on my back. I hunched my shoulders and slipped both hands, palms up, under my hanging belly. I lifted my paunch, measuring the fat. Every time I took a shower I checked how many fingers, or what fraction of a finger, was still visible as I peered down over my breasts and the gradual slope of my belly before it dropped off abruptly just above the

92

first outcropping of pubic hair. Now that my belly over-lapped my hands altogether, I tried to figure how far it stuck out past the sighting point. It was the strangest moment of any ordinary day, standing there using both hands to hold a piece of me that wasn't supposed to exist, wishing it gone. I shut off the water and pushed open the clouded glass door to reach for a towel.

Chapter
Ten

FELICE SENT ME ROCKS. SHE MAILED THEM in small boxes and padded envelopes, writing "F. Ventura" in bold fuschia letters as the return address. I had just walked in the door, jangling my keys and thinking that I was sick of the smell of myself in my white polyester tunic, but feeling too lazy to wash it again, when I saw a package on the coffee table, waiting for me.

Mom and Dad were in their bedroom watching TV, neglecting the big color console in the living room in favor of stretching out on their bed in their bathrobes, watching "McMillan and Wife." They had a happy marriage.

Mom called hello down the hall. I knew if she heard me walk into the kitchen, she'd probably come out to keep an eye on me, so I yelled hello back and unwrapped the package standing right there, all pulse and clumsy fingers. Even with nobody watching, I was a little embarrassed to be so excited. It meant more than a rock usually would.

I had tried putting all the rocks Felice sent in an egg carton with labels, so they would pass for a hobby, but it turned out that I was much happier scattering them or piling them in heaps. I liked touching them a lot more than I cared about writing down their names. I was learning their names, though. Felice had sent me rhodenite, chrysocolla, plume agate, apatized jasper, and petrified wood. She would always enclose a scrap of paper giving the name of the rock and the place she found it: Plume Agate, Chacra Mesa. Sometimes she stuck in a letter. Once she mailed a piece of glass that was lavender from lying eighty years in the sun. The letter she sent with this package read:

Dear Char:

Just got back from a run, took a shower, and felt like writing you. Been running a lot, burning off fat. Feels good. I do it mornings on Highway 35. There's not much shoulder, but not many cars go by. This morning, though, a cop car came up next to me and slowed down. I tried to run faster, but the guy kept driving right at my pace, staring at me through his dark glasses. Finally he went on by. It was weird.

Another thing happened on my run this morning—I found this rock. I looked it up in my *Geology Pocket Crammer.* Think it's chalcedony. Says here it's a beautiful quartz material with a red, waxy luster, chiefly found filling or lining cracks and cavities in igneous rock. Maybe they cracked open a vein of it when they built the road.

I'm sending it to you. Hope' things are going okay. Write soon.

Love,

Felice

I carried the letter and the chalcedony with me into the bathroom. It was a small pinkish-red wedge of rock. When I held it up to the light, I could see through the edges. The color almost pulsed, like the red you see when you close your eyes in bright sun. I took off my tunic and ran cold water over my wrists to help me cool off.

I set the chalcedony on the nightstand next to my alarm clock and looked at it before I fell asleep. The rest of the rocks from Felice were heaped around it. Some spilled over onto the floor, but none of them were lost.

THAT LITTLE PIECE of chalcedony was in my pocket at work the next day when Peg and Ginny and I decided to have dinner together. I wasn't quite sure how it happened. It was breaking a taboo, something like tickling the usher at the movies when he held out his hand to take your ticket. Not too serious, but not proper. It wasn't the first time aides and patients had crossed the line, of course. Everyone knew the story about John the orderly kissing Hannah Schneider.

With Peg and Ginny and me, it was only dinner. It was a long July evening, so we ate in the courtyard after I finished my shift. I went out and bought watermelon and pizza. Ginny contributed tomatoes from her windowsill plants. Peg got full bowls from the salad bar, and we pulled out the rusty lettuce and the pithiest radishes to feed to the birds. The grackles snatched the food that spilled from Peg's plate as she ate. Her hands were shaking quite a lot that night. She wore a loose t-shirt and

97

jean cutoffs. Ginny had on a floaty green shawl, with a pattern of roses threaded through it, over a cotton tank top. I could see the strong muscles in her shoulders and the slack parts of her arms that she couldn't use. I had done her nails that afternoon, so they glinted in the soft evening light. For a minute the color looked like the color of chalcedony, even though I knew the label on the bottle said "Magenta Dream."

Ginny's sister Lilah had come about a week ago and stayed for hours putting Ginny's hair in corn rows for coolness and pride. Ginny told me that the pattern made her a princess, then beckoned me over. She reached up and used her knuckles to push back some loose hair which had escaped from my own regulation pony tail. She had a light touch. I flushed and felt flattered.

We sat in the evening breeze, eating and talking about horoscopes, movies, Iris's past mysteries and present temper. "Still getting acquainted with pain," said Ginny, "and they aren't hitting it off."

"Nobody hits it off with pain," said Peg, taking a big, sloppy bite of pizza.

I put the watermelon on the stone bench and carved into it with a knife. Ginny was busy talking. "I'll never forget my first day here," she said, drawing the shawl up around her bare shoulders. "I was straight out of the hospital, and before that, two years of living with my family, sitting in front of soap operas, watching Mama talk with my sisters on the phone." Ginny jiggled her plate, and the pizza crusts rattled against each other. "One thing about Mama, she makes the world's best biscuits, all hot and flaky under gravy. I never get anything like that around here."

"Yeah," Peg said, "but those biscuits wouldn't still be hot by the time you managed to get one to your mouth."

They laughed. I could almost see their slowness unfolding between them.

The breeze was moving in Peg's hair. "You were probably missing that husband of yours the whole time you were at home," she said. I pulled out the knife and the watermelon opened with a snapping sound.

Ginny handed me her plate. "There were a lot of gaps in my life. I was used to spark." Peg nodded like she was hearing something she already knew. Ginny looked at me. "I had applied for public housing and found out there was no way I'd get a spot while I was living at home. People coming out of institutions get priority, and nobody else ever gets in. So when I got sick, I decided to come here and get on the waiting list for an apartment."

I was cutting small, dripping chunks of melon for Peg, flicking the seeds out with the edge of the knife. "And you've been here for years?" I licked my fingers. They were slick and sweet.

"The list is years long." Peg snorted. "It's a disgrace. I'm on it, too." She went after the melon with a fork, frowning in concentration. "I remember you coming in, Ginny, a tomato plant in your lap, surrounded by serious sisters and their laughing children. Every one of them was trying to keep a hand on you as you wheeled down the hall."

I cut a firm red piece out of the heart for Ginny. She was sitting with a very straight back. "Lilah took one look around and said, 'Not enough color in this place.' I had to tell her for the fifty-third time that it was only a temporary arrangement."

I gave Peg another piece with rind. "Then what happened?"

Ginny was speaking softly. "They checked me in, unpacked and set up the room the way I wanted it, with my plants at the window and my fringed lamp next to the bed. We all cried with the door shut, then my family left.

"At dinner that night I sat next to a black-haired, red-faced woman who smiled and said, 'Could I ask the spelling of your name?'

"I spelled it for her, none too friendly, and she wrote it down. She said she wanted to feature me in her memoirs. Cool as a cucumber." Ginny leaned toward Peg in the present. "Bold as brass."

Everything looked lovely to me. There was a summer dusk light on both of their faces. Peg skidded a hunk of melon off her tray into Ginny's lap, laughing. Ginny bent and ate it with no hands, straight from the rind.

THE NEXT MORNING was Sunday. I woke up feeling religious for a change, so I put on my pink dress and went with Mom to the early service. I didn't stay to help her with Sunday School, but came home to get dinner on the table. Mom went to church to hang out with the two- and three- and four-year-olds. She clapped hands with them and sang small songs. Sometimes she would bring whipping cream and let them make butter. She told them Bible stories that turned out to be about sharing or helping mother at home.

I didn't like kids. For me, church was a social challenge. This morning my church friend Marcie whispered to me that I had white stuff on my mouth. In the cramped ladies room mirror, I found out that it was excess toothpaste from brushing my teeth so extravagantly before I had come to worship. I couldn't think why Mom had let me out of the house like that, unless she had her mind on playtime ahead.

I walked in our front door after church feeling depressed. The sun was pouring in the big front windows, making bright splashes on the green carpet. Dust was sparking and floating like chipped-off bits of light. No one else was home. Dad had gone to the late service and would be coming back with Mom in a couple of hours. Jeff was having his usual red-eyed weekend someplace else. I put the roast on to cook with potatoes and carrots and wandered back into the living room, kicking off my good shoes.

I went to the record rack and pulled out a couple of Dad's old LPs. I went jazz instead of country. Ella Fitzgerald. Jonah Jones.

Ella came on singing "Night in Tunisia." I liked the velvet in her voice behind the album's scratch. It moved me more than disco, except when I was with Felice. I did a few steps of the hard part of the dance she'd tried to teach me, but I couldn't really move. My clothes were too tight.

I walked down the hall to my room to take off my Sunday best. The pink dress made me feel almost pretty, but the pantyhose were awful. I was packed into them like meat in a sausage casing. They were queen-size, but the waistband caught under my stomach and the crotch only came halfway up my thighs. I tore the hose on my toenails taking them off. I pulled my dress and slip over my head, unhooked my bra, and stepped out of my underwear. I felt a shiver of self-consciousness, but it was a relief to be naked. Ella was singing, "Now you push the middle valve down, the music goes round and round, and it come out here." I picked up a handful of Felice's rocks from my nightstand and rolled them between my palms. Agate, jasper, gypsum, chalcedony, quartz, others. Slowly, I started moving to the music, still holding the rocks. The windows worried me. I imagined how flabby and ridiculous I'd look if someone peered in. I paused, but then I shook my shoulders and danced down the hall to the living room in a burst of defiance.

I did disco dance steps to the rest of Ella Fitzgerald. When Jonah Jones dropped, I stood in the spill of sunlight, grinding my hips to the trumpet. I started hiding rocks all over my body. I stuck quartz and gypsum under my breasts, then added chalcedony to the left one. Plenty of room, and they stayed up. I tucked a small, rough lump of pumice under the fold of my belly. I put agate and jasper and feldspar in the layers of my sides. I stopped swaying and went into a shimmy. The agate fell out and bounced off my hip onto the floor. The rocks rubbed against me, feeling cool, but I was working up a sweat. I imagined smuggling jewels or drugs in my fat. It was almost exotic, not just a ruby in the navel, but quartz under the breasts, gypsum in the side pockets, pumice in the paunch place. I felt wicked and dreamy. I closed my eyes, still rolling with the music. My mind rippled out to Ginny and Peg.

I kept dancing, thinking, Oh Ginny, oh Ginny, oh Peg, oh, dropping rocks all around me to the music of the muted trumpet. Ginny kisses Peg. I know she does. She must. They do. I know it. I've seen them rubbing arms. That's for real. They lean forward in their chairs and they kiss. It's reliable. They wheel their chairs away from the hallway into Ginny's room, with Elvis loving me tender and a soft lamp shutting out the harsh overheads. It's got to happen.

I couldn't believe it.

I rolled my hips in the other direction and lost the pumice. They really kiss? How do they kiss? Who can lean forward enough? Perez must help. She gives Peg a hand onto Ginny's bed, raises the rails, shuts the door. Or they have a foam pad somebody spreads out on the floor so they can roll around without getting hurt. Or maybe they go swimming on disability day at the YMCA pool and touch weightlessly, fighting chlorine and crowds instead of gravity. It's not just kissing. Maybe they do it sitting up, reaching under each other's clothes, tender. Or Peg rolls to Ginny's room at night, finds her way to the bed, and leans her face on the edge of the mattress. Her breasts press against the tight hospital corners of the sheet. Ginny braces herself on her elbows and moves on Peg's soft fist, rubbing. They are both silent because of the people sleeping all around them. Ginny and her body travel far, but she doesn't come. She's afraid to, because it might bring bladder spasms. Peg's face is intent as she lets her arm fall back into her lap. Ginny makes a slow turn on the bed, until she can kiss Peg's breasts through her shirt. Ginny unbuttons it with her teeth.

I barge in with plans for helping them, rescuing them. The trumpet was playing in spurts, higher and higher. I would risk my job. I would let Peg sleep with Ginny. Pretty crowded for two big women in a single bed, especially since they need pillows under their legs and to be turned in the night. Okay, I would push the beds together, since there was an extra in Ginny's room. They could have a makeshift double. I'd work it out so that Perez and I would have the night shift. Perez wouldn't tell, and nobody else needed to know. Mabel might notice that there was no Peg sleeping in their room, but Mabel wouldn't talk. Peg and Ginny would be so grateful. I'd be a hero. Humanitarian aid to the handicapped. Maybe someday they'd give me a plaque.

And what about getting fired? Well, I was quitting to go back to high school anyway in September. I didn't like to think about that, but it made losing this job not such a big deal. I'd hate to leave in disgrace, though. I'd be in big trouble, what would my mother say? And what about leaving, anyway; what would happen when I left? Maybe

Perez would do it then, but who could she be working with that she could count on not to squeal? Perez needed this job. Getting caught would be worse for her.

The record was over. I could smell the roast. Mom and Dad would be home soon. I had to stop and get dressed, but I closed my eyes and rolled my hips a minute longer, still dropping rocks and willing myself to risk my summer job for the secret part of the dream: the part where I got to slip in between Ginny and Peg in the railed bed and gather some of the warmth.

Chapter
Eleven

MOM ANSWERED THE PHONE. I WAS IN THE kitchen making lunch, and my hands were sticky with peanut butter and honey. She called up to me from the basement where she was doing laundry, "Char-lotte. It's Felice."

Her voice gave me a shiver, as if I was about to do something dangerous. I picked up the phone.

"Hi," said Felice. "This is going to be short."

I didn't know whether to be excited or disappointed, so I went for reserved. "OK," I said, wiping honey from the receiver with my sleeve.

We talked for an hour. Felice had a lot of stories to hint at, and I had a few myself. She screamed when I told her about Frank in Room 303 with the baby picture of himself he loved to show off to the aides, the one where his private part looked like a good length of garden hose.

I wanted to tell her about the food fight, and about Virgil, who had his legs cut off and tattoos on both stumps, but Mom came up from the basement to start peeling oranges for ambrosia, so I was reduced to grunts, uh-huhs, and you knows.

Then Felice said, "When are you coming out here? It would be fun to see you."

I said, "Next weekend."

She laughed. "Good."

"Really? You want me to come?"

"Yeah," said Felice. "Come."

Just like that, I was planning a trip. Felice had asked me to come. It made me feel like anything was possible. As soon as I got off the phone, I asked Mom if I could borrow the Pinto.

She was pouring shredded coconut from a bag into a white bowl. "To see Felice? That's an awfully long drive. Isn't she coming back in a few weeks?"

I whined. "Yeah, but I've been working all summer. I need a break. And I've never been to New Mexico."

She offered me a piece of orange. "Maybe your brother would go with you."

That was the last thing I needed. "Jeff already has plans for next weekend."

Mom hesitated, then said, "All right, Charlotte. You may borrow the car. Just be sure to call me when you get there. I trust you to be careful." I hugged her and opened the package of miniature marshmallows for her to stir into the fruit.

After that, it was easy. I collected on a summer of favors to get Friday to Monday off work. I skimmed through my short week. Mom packed me a lunch for the drive. It was a bologna sandwich in a baggie with mustard and only one slice of bread, along with some celery sticks and an apple. I looked at it when she handed it to me, and it jerked me right back into childhood. Felice used to split her Ding Dongs with me, since I never had sweets. I gave Mom a hug and carried the bag outside to finish cleaning the car.

I had already vacuumed it out, emptied the little wastebasket that straddled the hump, and taken Armor-all to the vinyl, so now I put the lunch bag down on the passenger seat, and went around to the front of the car to check the oil. Then I slammed the hood and got in on the driver's side.

"Goodbye." Mom was leaning from the door. "Be careful." She stepped out onto the sidewalk to see me off.

"Bye," I said. I waved my lunch bag at her. Then I pulled away from the curb. I glanced in the rearview mirror as she turned to say something to the dog.

I went decently slow through the neighborhood streets, but it wasn't far to the highway. Felice and I got on it here when we were heading downtown to cruise. I pulled onto the entrance ramp. It had a sharp curve that Felice said always tempted her to quit steering and let the car drift straight off the edge of the overpass. I thought of that every time I took the curve, trying the over-the-brink idea out on myself, but I didn't get it. Staying on the road felt good to me.

I loved to drive on the highway. It was so different from wading through the traffic lights on Moody Boulevard on the way to work, the ones timed to make you stop, then stop, then stop again. I liked fifty-five, felt strange and powerful at sixty, and didn't mind going seventy-five to pass. I loved the glove compartment and the map light and the stick shift. The only thing I didn't like was the seat belt, so I let it slip harmlessly down into the crack in the seat.

I was already past Castle Rock, making good time, feeling anonymous. It felt great. Everything out the window was moving. I watched the gray asphalt shoulder go wavery at the edges in the heat. I looked into cars as I passed them. I saw pillows jammed up against the window, tired kids making their troll dolls wave from the back seat. I blew them a kiss, then looked back at the road. Goodbye all that. I wished I could stick both feet out the window and keep one on the gas at the same time.

The Pinto got a vibration going over forty-five, but I turned the radio up and ignored it. I had the spectrum to choose from—pop to rock to light classical to talk—but I went country western.

> *Satin sheets to lie on*
> *Satin pillows to cry on*
> *Still, I'm not happy*
> *Don't you see…*

I hung on to the image: satin pillows, satin sheets. God, what all was possible in life? I even liked the market report, listening to the price of sugar beets and soy beans and trying to guess what was growing in the fields I was passing.

In Trinidad, I pulled into a Sinclair station to gas up. I picked up my lunch bag and carried it with me into the rest room. I wasn't sure what I had in mind. I unlocked the door with a key attached to a huge hunk of plastic that had "LADIES" on it in raised gold letters. I balanced the lunch bag on the edge of the chipped white sink. It immediately slipped down under the dripping faucet. I succumbed to impulse and twisted both handles to turn the water on full blast. The brown bag got darker and started to disintegrate. The baggie with the celery floated. The baggie with the sandwich filled with water and sank. It became awful to look at, so I turned off the water and let the sink drain. I scooped out the food with a brown paper towel and dropped it into the trash can. I saved the apple, though, rinsing it carefully before I scrubbed the sink with pink liquid soap from the dispenser. I finished my business, returned the key, paid, and, curiously light-headed, hit the road.

Driving felt like flying. I poured myself a Dixie cup full of ice water from the thermos at my feet. The radio was crackling, but

My D-I-V-O-R-C-E
becomes final
today

blew on through the static. I went straight up Raton Pass. The Pinto's engine was pulling and straining. As far as I was concerned, though, we had left the ground. I was far from home. I was on my own. I had a shiny red apple on the seat next to me. The radio kept at it:

I turned out to be
the only hell my mama
ever raised

Once the Pinto and I made it over the pass, we left other cars in the dust. They would appear in tight clumps of three or four together, and I would work my way into the lead. I stopped waving at the children and started noticing the women. Most were on the passenger side, so I saw more of their hairdos than their faces. One woman in a town car with a pink sweater and a bald driver-husband was in the act of turning to speak with her backseat children, and our eyes met. Her face seemed to startle then soften as we looked at each other, then she said something into the side of her husband's neck, and he turned to stare at me. I hit the gas.

Something had gotten into me. It must have been white-line fever. Even the apple on the seat beside me looked heightened, redder than any apple I had ever seen, special. I didn't feel like eating it, but I was starting to get hungry.

The next little town, Maxwell, had a peeling-paint restaurant right off the highway, so I pulled into the parking lot. I tried to remember if I had ever eaten at a restaurant by myself before, and the answer was no, not a sit-down dinner. I combed my hair in the rearview mirror and decided that I'd leave the waitress an extra dollar if she called me honey. I might even say that her dress was pretty or that she was pretty. My heart stopped pounding as soon as I saw her, because she was younger than me, maybe fifteen, and a blonde. She looked a lot like my ninth-grade locker partner. She was beaming, leaning over a booth, and talking to a woman in her sixties. It turned out the older woman was her grandmother, and the waitress was showing her off to the woman behind the cash register, who had "Louise" embroidered over her pocket. The grandmother got up to help clear the table, and she made a crack about keeping the tip. The waitress turned to Louise. "Isn't she a riot?" She meant it. The two of them were gloating over each other. Louise was swatting flies and drinking tea.

The waitress came over to take my order after her grandmother left. She called me Ma'am. I noticed the Waist Watcher's beef patty and cottage cheese special, but I didn't feel my usual urge to scrunch up my shoulders when I asked for barbecued chicken and a baked potato with sour cream and butter. I just said it, and she wrote it down and brought it to me with a tossed salad. I thought of how much Peg would enjoy this meal. The waitress and Louise settled themselves on stools on opposite sides of the counter.

I ate my dinner. It was good. It wasn't until I stood up to walk to the restroom that I began to get an inkling of what was happening. It was a little like walking out into a dark night from a bright room; at first I was disoriented, but by the time I reached for the faucet in the restroom, I had a grasp on it. I washed my face in the sink and looked in the mirror. I wasn't dieting. I nodded. I wasn't. The walls were pink plaster. There was graffiti knifed into the wooden stalls, all names and hearts. Louise was mentioned. I thought maybe I was having a revelation, which didn't seem like something I could saunter out and mention to the waitress when she brought me the bill. I couldn't drop a revelation as small talk to Louise when I tossed a penny mint on the counter to add to my bill. Or maybe I could, maybe I should tell people with just that casualness, but I thought I'd better start with someone I knew. So I left Louise and the waitress talking about the cook, who was practically a shut-in, and got back on the road.

It still felt good to be in the car. I felt safe and completely alone. The highway narrowed to two lanes, and I got a warm glow thinking about how I didn't have a station wagon full of family with me: Jeff wasn't rapping me on the head with his knuckles; Mom wasn't glancing over her shoulder to be sure I had my seatbelt fastened; I was in the driver's seat. My eyes were tired, but there weren't many cars coming at me. The big trucks crossed the solid yellow line to pass. I turned off the air conditioning and rolled down the windows. I didn't have to think about myself or any new truths. I could keep my eyes on the road and let the night air brush across the flat land and on over me.

Chapter
Twelve

I KEPT DRIVING, FINALLY TIRED. I THOUGHT of pulling into a rest stop for a nap, but I didn't want to wake up with my face drooling on the vinyl. I wanted to get there. I was at the town limits before I realized that I hadn't spent any time on the trip dreaming of Felice. It gave me a guilty start, and I was suddenly wide awake, craning to read street signs and trying to figure out my directions in the faint map light.

I was coming in at the end of the long summer dusk. A gray light was bringing out the shadows of the houses as I passed. I stopped in front of a small two-story house with a cactus planter next to the front steps and spiky yucca lining the walk. I got out of the car, pushed my hair out of my eyes, and stood there blinking. Kids in the next yard were playing a wild game of swinging statue, the bigger ones throwing the smaller ones across the thin lawn. I carried my backpack up the steps and knocked on the frame of the latched screen door. Nobody came, so I called, "Hello?" No answer. I raised my voice. "Hello, is anybody home?" I could see a full ashtray next to the brown couch, but still nobody came. I laid my head back and screamed, "Felice!"

The neighbor kids stopped throwing each other around and looked at me in dead silence. Through the silence I heard a rustling, then Felice came running around from the back of the house. She jumped over an abandoned big wheel scooter and threw her arms around me. Lord, she felt good. She pulled back and pointed out her tan and the muscles in her legs. I laughed at how proud she was of them there in the half dark. We hugged again before we walked up the front steps into the house.

We looked at each other under the hall light. She had on a yellow tank top and her hair had lightened in the sun. For a minute, I missed scabby-kneed Felice, who had the seven-year-old courage to be friends with me when I was a teacher's pet who had trouble getting my clothes on right-side-out.

She took my backpack and tossed it onto the couch. It jostled the ashtray, causing a small cloud of silver ash to rise. "Let's go dancing," she said.

I didn't say I was exhausted. I said, "Is there some-place we can get in?"

"We can try." Felice took me out to the patio and introduced me to her cousin Mickey, who was sitting in a lawn chair drinking a Schlitz and watching her son kick a blow-up wading pool across the yard.

Mickey gave me a big smile and said, "That's Kenny doing soccer practice. He's nine. You'll meet my husband Rick later, when he gets off work. Did Felice show you where to find sheets and towels?" I noticed that I could see her ribs through her bodysuit.

Felice picked up her own can of Schlitz from the painted metal table. "Mickey, she just got here. We're going out."

Kenny lofted the wading pool high in the air, obviously aiming for Felice's head, but she stuck out her arm and punched it away. "Cut it out," she said mildly.

I looked up at the moon, still arriving. The stars were easing into brightness. I found the Big Dipper and tried to get my bearings. Wet plastic slapped me in the face. Kenny had scored with the wading pool.

Mickey threw her cigarette pack at the kid, but it fell short. Kenny was giggling and racing around the clothesline. "Excuse me," said Mickey, "but I guess somebody needs to be rescued from hysteria. You girls have fun."

Felice changed into a pair of jeans and a white shirt. I put on jeans, too, and a big pink blouse, which I left unbuttoned two buttons lower than Mom would have found decent. I knew I might be too tired to have fun, but I was already in a daze as if I'd had three or four beers, so it might work out. If we made it into the bar, of course. Felice had extracted Mickey's expired learner's permit from her. It didn't have a picture, but it said I was twenty-seven and weighed 120 pounds. Felice thought it might slide by. The other problem was that she was using Mickey's current driver's license, so we had to go in separately and just hope that they didn't notice we both had the same name and address.

I was amazed when it worked. Felice went in first, grinned at the doorman, and didn't get carded. I sat in the car in the parking lot for about ten minutes before braving the door myself. I already had my hand on my ID, and I sort of thrust it at the guy when he looked at me. He pulled out his flashlight to read it. "Bring something better next time," he said, handing it back.

We were in. The lights were dim, the carpet was red, and the only table in the place was taken by three loud cowboys and a woman in a black velvet vest. Everyone else was either at the bar or leaning against a rail watching the dancers. The music sounded electronic and strange to me. I'd lost touch with the hot dance songs while Felice had been gone. I looked around for her, finally spotting her on the dance floor. Her white shirt reflected red, then blue, then violet as the lighting changed, and she was doing a fast version of the dance steps we had worked on in her living room all last spring. The guy she was dancing with had blond hair, black jeans, and a sense of rhythm that left me in the dust. They were smooth; they'd done this before. I hoped she would quit after just one song. I bought myself a beer and circled the dance floor a couple of times, looking for a place to lean, feeling huge. I finally wedged myself into a spot on the rail next to one of the enormous speakers, with good views of both Felice and the door. The song was laced with police whistles, and every time one sounded, I kept thinking the place was getting busted and the underaged drinkers would be hauled off to jail. So I kept one eye on the door as I stood there soaking up cigarette smoke, watching the men operate, and watching Felice do the part where they held hands and turned back to back. She spun out, and he caught her with his arm around her waist. They got all excited that they'd done it right and smiled at each other.

When the song was done, Felice looked around for me. She waved, said goodbye to her partner, and came over. She said she'd seen him here before, and leaned up close to take of sip of my drink. "Mmm, that tastes good," she said, and she was off to buy herself one. I gave her money to get me another beer, too. The speaker was too loud for much thinking, but I did manage to wish that we'd gone someplace quieter where we could talk. Felice was one for action, though. I leaned and waited. She came back red-faced and excited after four or five songs. She was trying to tell me what some guy had said to her on the way to the bar, how she'd had to duck into the women's room to get rid of him, but I couldn't hear what she was saying. We settled into leaning and staring at the dancers until Donna Summer came on. "Bad Girls." That was a song I could get behind. Felice jumped up and put her arm on my shoulder. She wanted me to dance with her. I was trying to decide if I could be that exposed in this crowd, when Mr. Black Jeans came up behind her and took hold of her elbow. She nodded at him, smiled at me, and was back out on the floor, looking elegant and wild.

I went to the bar to buy myself a screwdriver. I drank it fast, got my hand stamped by the door man, and went out to the parking lot to throw up. I rinsed my mouth with water from my car thermos. The building thumped with amplified bass. I leaned on the Pinto and cried. This had happened before on nights out with Felice. Discos made me sad.

Felice and I never did dance together, but we did talk a little on the ride home. She told me about her job—how she stood in the back of the restaurant scraping bean pots and lard buckets. "It's so hot back there," she said. "I almost never wear makeup anymore because it would sweat right off." The job had its good points, though: she got to drink all the pop she wanted, this guy Tony told jokes and gave her joints, and sometimes he reached around her from behind while she was doing dishes. One night he sprayed her with the black hose they used to rinse the vegetables, and they had a big water fight.

"Don't look so worried, Char," she said, rolling down the car window. "It's just a work thing." By the time we got home, we were so tired that I put on my sleeping t-shirt and dropped into Felice's double bed without feeling much tension, and she crawled in beside me without taking off her make-up or taking a shower. We slept.

I WOKE BEFORE Felice, feeling unreasonably happy. My head was aching, but it was morning and I was hungry. That made me smile. I hadn't told Felice about my new state of grace. State of grace. I laughed into the pillow. I knew it wasn't safe to talk to Felice about not dieting, because I'd seen the pudgy picture of herself up on the refrigerator and the cottage cheese and grapefruit on the shelves. Still, I was feeling good, so I hugged the pillow and imagined getting up and cooking breakfast for Felice. I'd do it quietly, right there in her cousin's strange kitchen.

I'd find a pan to bake some biscuits. I'd use a dusted glass to roll them out if Mickey didn't have a jelly jar, then I'd cut the dough into thin, perfect circles. I'd lift them, white and powdery, onto the pan, bake them in a hot oven until I could pull them out light and fragrant, and pile them in a basket with a blue checkered cloth. I'd slit a few and touch them with butter that would be melted when Felice stumbled in, drawn out of bed by the warm smell. I'd have honey and apple jelly already by her plate, each with a spoon waiting to dip in and daub on her choice of sweetness. I'd pour her a tall, cold glass of orange juice as she sat down, and slip eggs scrambled with milk and cheese and sage, and sprinkled with bits of green pepper, onto her plate. There would be peaches in a white bowl in the middle of the table. Even before she was fully awake, her mouth would be caught with biscuit and honey, and light, hot eggs, opening to flavors she would have been afraid to ask for, things so good that she would look at me and be amazed that I had made them.

And in that simple moment of her pleasure, I, my mother's daughter, would set my own plate at the table. I would heap it full of eggs, and three biscuits, two with honey, one with jelly. I would take smooth gulps of milk. I would split a peach with her, pulling it, wet and sweet, off the pit. I would look at Felice with juice dripping from my lips, and I would say, "It's good." She would nod with her mouth full, her own lips sticky with honey and biscuit crumbs. She would swallow and take a sip from her glass before she reached across the table to cover my hand with hers. "Very good."

I giggled so hard that I slobbered on the pillowcase. "Young Betty Crocker." Felice rolled over onto her side, her flat, abrupt back to me. I felt her irritation at my noises, but I couldn't help laughing again. I was delighted with myself at that moment, big, sloppy body, bar breath, and all. The sun was hitting my thighs. They were out from under the rumpled sheet, and I looked at them, wide and white and loose in the sunlight. I patted them as if they were large, friendly dogs.

I'd had enough hallucinations for one morning, so I got out of bed. Felice put the pillow over her head and curled up in a tight ball, distinctly like someone who didn't want to be told good morning. I pulled on my jeans and wandered out to the kitchen, where Mickey and Kenny were reading the backs of cereal boxes. Mickey offered me some unfrosted strawberry Pop Tarts. I laughed and popped them into the toaster to warm.

Felice came out, eventually, wet from the shower and not hungry. I hadn't seen her eat a meal since I'd arrived. She wrestled the paper away from Kenny and checked the movie listings. Nothing exciting was happening in town that day, so we decided to go camping. We borrowed a red tent, a sleeping bag, a pot, and a bunch of blankets from Mickey. She helped us dump everything into the back of the Pinto. Felice showed me the way to the supermarket, where we bought peanut butter, bread, Doritos, hot chocolate mix, and matches, along with the traditional grocery store six-pack of beer. I added apples and a block of cheese.

"Listen to this," said Felice as we stood in the express line. "'New-born baby threatens Mom with gun. Doctor hands over wallet.'" She was reading aloud from a tabloid with a picture of Cher on the cover.

"'I was driven to crime by labor pains,' confesses tot," I improvised over her shoulder.

There was no trouble at the cash register over the six-pack. Felice had a bottle of peppermint schnapps that she had lifted from Mickey's liquor cabinet, and I had some pot, so we were all set.

I let Felice drive as we headed south. She didn't want to have to do any map reading, and I never liked driving as much when Felice was with me. She was always bouncing all over the radio dial, opening beers, and taking off sweaters. It distracted me.

We drove for hours, singing all of our old cruising songs. "Delta Dawn" had never sounded so melancholy and harmonious. I trailed my hand out the window, making small motions to follow the outlines of the telephone poles and the mountains in the distance. Sometimes my hand ran flat across the desert for a while. We tried singing, "What's the Buzz," but that was all we knew of the words, so we dragged out "Last Dance," "I Love the Night Life," and "Weekend Lover" before we settled into drinking our beers and reliving the night I had drunk myself sick at the drive-in on bottled tequila sunrises. Felice and Tim had had to carry me into the house and dump me in bed, then they had gone out to Sambo's. That was when Tim had made his move on Felice. That story made me too queasy to be good car talk, so I brought up the time Felice had dropped her quartz key chain out of the car window on Moody Boulevard. We had pulled over and made dashes between the cars to look for it. Felice had found it just as the cops pulled up, but we didn't get arrested. We just explained.

We finally broke open the Doritos, and Felice pointed across the flat, sagebrush plain to a breast-shaped peak all alone against the horizon. "That's got to be a volcano," she said. "I think these fields are pumice. That's why not much grows here. Not enough soil has built up. The rock is too new. Look at the map."

It took me a while to figure out where we were, but she was right. Mount Estrella, extinct volcano. There was a state campground at the top. About halfway up Mt. Estrella we drove through a camping area packed with RVs and families. We continued past it on an unmarked, rutted dirt road that Felice insisted would take us to the top. It was slow going, even before it began to rain. She turned on the windshield wipers. I started to panic.

"Felice, this road isn't going anywhere." I fastened my seatbelt.

Felice cracked her window to let a little air into the car. Rain blew in. "Where do you think I could turn around?" The trees were tight on one side of us, and a river had cut a deep gulley on the other. She was right. The only thing we could do was get to where ever the road was going.

It ended at another campsite, empty except for us. Felice parked the Pinto next to a picnic table, and we sat in the car for a minute looking out through the windshield at the trees leaning in the rain. They were tall, skinny firs, and they bent and shook and creaked against each other. We ate some more Doritos. I tried to launch into "Bridge Over Troubled Waters," but it wasn't really in our repertoire. Felice turned around and started rummaging in the back seat.

"We better set up the tent," she said.

I looked at the rain bouncing off the red-stained wood of the picnic table. "Couldn't we wait until it stops?"

She had the bag with the tent in her lap. "It might be dark by then."

We put on our jackets and got out of the car. The rain was alternating between driving sheets and a fine mist. We got to work. Felice had put this tent up before, so it didn't take us long to get it raised and staked down. Then I ran with the sleeping bag and blankets from the car to the tent, kneeling in the tent door to spread them out, blocking the rain with my back. When I went back for the food and the backpacks, Felice had pulled my snowdrift shovel out from under the seat.

"We have to dig a trench around the tent so the rain has someplace to drain," she said, her face dripping.

That didn't sound like anything I would have expected Felice to know. "Where did you hear that?"

She pushed the blade into the ground with her tennis shoe. "White Sands," she said, and I realized it had to have come from Tony.

There was only one shovel, so I went and sat in the car. I didn't want to get the inside of the tent all wet, but I felt cramped and close in the Pinto. Felice worked steadily, and I could see the muscles in her back tightening as she lifted each shovelful of dirt. She looked strangely fragile to me as she dug. After a while I went out and took the shovel. She went to the car and came back without her wet jacket, in just her t-shirt and shorts. The ground was heavy, and it stuck to the shovel. I only hit one rock. It was big and flat. Felice got into the trench and pushed from below, while I pried from above.

After we lifted it out, the rock left a hole much deeper than the rest of the trench. Felice smoothed the edges of the hole with her hands, filling it in so the water wouldn't stop there. I finished the trench. When I looked through the mist at the Pinto, it looked odd, almost like an artifact from another time. I remembered that Mom used to tell me a storm was a giant rolling a wheelbarrow full of potatoes across the sky. The lightning was sparks from its wheels, and thunder was potatoes falling from the cart.

I slogged over to where Felice was working. She looked at me. "You're filthy."

I huddled down knee to knee with her and drew her initials in the mud on her thigh. "You're worse."

She scooped up a handful of dirt and slung it at me. It hit my stomach where it hung over the snap of my jeans. I took a step back and tripped over the shovel. I almost fell, but grabbed a tree and hung on, splattering Felice with more mud in the process. She reached to give me a hand, and we both lost our footing, so we were sitting there laughing and spitting dirt and water when the late afternoon sun came out.

Things warmed and dried out fast in the sharp sun. Felice wanted to follow a footpath to the very top of the volcano, but I needed to wash. So she headed up, and I walked down to a wide place in the river. The water was very cold, full of new rain and snowmelt runoff. I gasped when I stuck my foot in, but it quickly went numb, so I took off my jeans and my shirt and waded into the river in my underpants, in case anyone came. I shivered and bent to splash the sides of my calves and scrub the dirt off of my hands and arms. The bite of the cold softened enough that I lay down in the current, holding onto a rock, with my legs floating out from under me, and my hair spread out on the current. I floated there, with the cold water playing over me, looking up over the tops of the trees at the sudden blue sky and the frankly sinking sun. The implications of nightfall set in, and I pulled my feet back in under me and stood up to walk to the bank, all clumsy with cold. Felice was sitting next to my clothes, watching me, one hand trailing in the water and a hunk of obsidian balancing on her knee.

"Volcanic glass," she said as she handed me my t-shirt. She leaned to rinse her face in the river while I dried and dressed.

We gathered wood to make a fire. It caught just as we lost the sun. We tried toasting cheese sandwiches on sticks, but they dropped their cheese and burnt. We used Mickey's pot to heat up water for hot chocolate mixed with peppermint schnapps. I told Felice about the giant who makes the storms, and she told me that lava can flow up from a fissure in a cornfield with an explosion that can be heard several hundred miles away. Sometimes volcanic ash shoots up to a height of thirty miles, and the ash in the air reddens the sunset all around the world.

She said volcanoes erupt at places of weakness in the earth's crust. I put some pot in the pipe and lit it while she tried to explain how the highs and lows of the earth's surface are in equilibrium, even though mountains are constantly eroding and dumping soil into the low places. We kept passing the pipe. I didn't quite follow, but I liked to think of everything shifting, mountains crumbling down into valleys, which cracked open to spill out new rock to become another mountain. A volcano changes everything. It makes a new landscape, complete with lava rivers that crust over hard and black and shiny as glass. I took another sip of chocolate, but it made my stomach remember the night before, so I decided to stick to pot. When Vesuvius went off, Pompeii was buried in ash within thirty hours.

The fire was burning low, and I was getting cold. The stars were cracking the sky. We threw dirt on the fire and crawled into the tent.

We wrapped ourselves in blankets and huddled together under the sleeping bag. I turned on the flashlight and filled the pipe again. The air smelled slightly musty, as if the tent had been damp the last time it had been folded up. The dirt was soft under the ground cloth. The moon was shining through the skin of the tent, and it lit the bones and shadows of Felice's face with a filtered red light.

She was pulling on some long underwear under the blanket, but she kept her jacket on, too. "It's freezing," she said, and took a long hit from the pipe. I noticed how red her hands were as she held it. I could hear the river, and a stubborn crackling from the smothered fire.

"Now, wait," I said, sitting on my own hands to warm them, "there are three kinds of rocks, right? Igneous, and what else?"

"Sedimentary and metamorphic." Felice flopped down on her stomach and rested her chin on her hunk of obsidian. "All kinds of rocks. Chalk, flint, chert, marl, oolites, peat, coal, limestone." She took a drag on the pipe after every rock, so limestone came out with a cloud of smoke and coughs.

I took the pipe out of her hand and relit it. It tasted harsh, almost gone. "Would you know all of those rocks if you saw them?"

Felice sipped her cold hot chocolate. "Sure, I'd know them. If I didn't know them by looking, I'd smell them, taste them, check their color and luster. Try to break them—that's called cleavage. Scratch them with a penny. Then I could figure it out."

I put the pipe down in the lid from the peanut butter jar. Felice picked it up, dumped the ash, and started filling it again, all without sitting up.

I watched her fingers work and started imagining them held curled and tight together, like Peg's. It was like identifying rocks, I thought. I could tell Felice from Peg by her hands. I got dreamy thinking about the qualities that identified my friends. Smell was easy—Felice smelled of opium oil, Peg smelled of new sweat when I was close, lifting her. Ginny smelled of Chantilly perfume. Maybe Peg tasted salty. Ginny tasted like lipstick, cakey; Felice tasted like peppermint and chocolate tonight. Color, color. Peg was red and flushed. Ginny was caramel. Felice was light toast brown, china white underneath. I said their qualities of luster out loud: "Peg shines, Ginny shines, Felice shines."

"What?" Felice had the pipe going again. She had scooted right up next to me to offer it.

"What kind of rock do you think I am?" I took the pipe, put a hand on her back, and rubbed her jacket up and down.

She put her head down and closed her eyes. "I don't know."

I went on to trying to figure out cleavage, which seemed abstract. How would they break? I decided Peg broke in chunks, each piece big enough to be a rock in itself. There was more to cleavage, though: Peg had small, down-looking breasts. Ginny broke into crystals. Her breasts were large and loose. Felice held out against breaking: maybe she was like lava and had to harden to crack. I looked at the one breast I could see from where I was sitting. It was squashed into the floor of the tent, since she was lying on it, but I knew it was small, and generally pointed up.

"Earth calling Char," said Felice. I got embarrassed, and Felice started talking about living with Mickey, Rick and Kenny—how Rick always had to work double shifts at the store, and how Mickey listened through the wall with a glass dipped in water whenever Rick went into the bedroom and shut the door to talk on the phone. While Felice was talking, we edged closer and closer together. I leaned my head down to hers to keep the pipe lit. Felice started rolling the obsidian up and down on her legs under her palm, then it slipped off between us, where our thighs were touching. She reached for it, and then we were kissing. She did taste like chocolate and peppermint. Her hands were tangled up in my hair, and the zipper of her jacket was digging into my skin where my sweater had ridden up. I reached out to pull the sleeping bag tight around us. Felice pushed her hands up under my shirt. They were warm. I wasn't cold at all anymore. I heard the rain start up again, hitting the tent, and smelled wet dirt. Felice took her jacket and sweater off. I wrapped my arms around her and just held on.

When she unfastened my jeans and inched the tight zipper down, I lifted my hips to help her. She pulled off my jeans and my underpants, stroking me as she went. I held my breath when her hand touched my belly ledge, as if it could stop everything, but she just moved on down my legs, careful not to leave my clothes hanging around my ankles. Then she followed her hands back up the soft insides of my thighs. I felt one finger circling with her dancer's rhythm, tracing the length of the folded place; then the finger lifted, went lightly to the top, and traced my edges again. The finger slid a little, wet now. I could feel her concentration through everything else I was feeling. She put both hands on the outer folds and held them apart. I heard her pull in a deep quick breath, as before a wonder, and say, "Chalcedony."

I didn't hear what else she whispered as she lowered her face to me, but she shaped my heart forever by releasing that one word. I knew it then.

Chapter Thirteen

I WAS COLD WHEN I WOKE UP. AIR WAS SLIPPING in under the edges of the sleeping bag. The rain flap was up, and I could see the white-gray sky through the door screen. Felice was gone.

I lay curled up tight against the morning until I had to get up to pee. By then, the sky was blue. As soon as I crawled out of the tent, I saw a rock on the picnic table, holding down a slip of white paper. It was a largish, brownish rock, with some odd knobs and a shiny place. The note had nothing to do with the rock, though. It said:

> Char—
>   Gone running. Took the left fork. Meet me at the bottom.
>   Love,
>   Felice

I folded up the paper and put it in the pocket of my jeans. I went and squatted under a Douglas fir, then came back and sat down on the picnic table bench. I thought about starting a fire to heat water for hot chocolate, but remembered that it would be dangerous to leave anything burning. I went to the tent and found the peanut butter jar with its ashy lid, scooped out a fingerful of peanut butter, and sucked it down to the nut bits, which I swallowed as a group. I kicked dirt over the black wood of last night's fire, just to be safe, and got in the car to go after Felice. I put the knobby rock on the floor of the backseat as a keepsake.

I looked wild in the rearview mirror. My hair was snarled with leaves and sticks, I had a smear of ash across my forehead, my glasses were dirty, and I thought maybe my lips had changed shape. I bared my teeth at myself, then turned on the engine, not displeased with the effect. All those years of braces had paid off.

I hadn't even noticed the left fork of the road. It split off just below the entrance to our campsite, and looked steeper and even more rocky than the one we had driven up. I hoped it didn't get any worse. The Pinto shook and thumped over gullies and ridges that testified to last night's storm, as well as years of runoff from the spring snowmelt.

I was mad that Felice had left me to go running. She should have stayed with me, so we could drowse into the morning side of last night. As it was, I would have to see her from far away, doing something I couldn't understand—running down a mountain. The distance made me feel bereft, but I figured the feeling was temporary.

I was jolted with every rut. I looked out the window. The trees were impassive. They belonged together. Felice had told me that their pine cones didn't open until there was a forest fire, and new seed was needed. The heat triggered it. Otherwise, the trees stood calmly undertaking their chemistry, making sugar from water and air, bending green needles in the breeze, allowing birds and squirrels to take vulgar animal liberties.

The wheels of the Pinto hesitated over a deep hole, but we made it without getting stuck. The ground began to level, and the trees were thinning. As I rounded a curve, the desert opened out flat in front of me.

I could see Felice. She looked like a pop-up greeting card against the flat blue sky. The land had quickly forgotten trees. It was all sage and outcroppings of black pumice. Felice was the only thing moving in the morning heat.

The Pinto stopped rattling and bucking. The surface of the road had changed, and I was driving on a wide, smooth black ribbon that stretched out in front of me as far as the eye could see. It shimmered in the sun. It looked new, which seemed odd, since there was no other sign of people, not even telephone poles.

I was getting closer to Felice. She was running slow, stretching her legs. She looked like she could go on forever like the road. I almost wished she would, so I could keep driving behind her at just this distance, watching her in the sharpening sun. I kept getting closer, though. She had pulled her hair back into a ponytail that barely shook as she ran, her stride was so smooth.

I saw her stumble. At first, I thought she was bending down to pick up a rock on the road, but I felt a tremor. The silver thermos on the floor of the front seat bounced up and hit me on the knee. Cracks opened in the asphalt before me, as if something were pushing up from inside the ground. I looked back at the mountain in the rearview mirror. There was no smoke, nothing but calm and trees.

Felice had gotten up and was running toward me. She was moving fast now, her face red with effort and fear. I noticed again how beautiful she was, before I gathered myself enough to hit the gas. When I reached her, I slammed on the brakes and opened the door. She scrambled in, gasping for breath. I spun the car around and started back onto the narrow dirt road that a moment ago had been wobbling like a board bridge in the wind.

Felice picked up the thermos, tilted her head back, and drank. The ground had stopped trembling, but her hands were shaking. So were mine. I split my attention between watching her throat move and getting us back up the mountain. They seemed of equal importance.

"Fasten your seatbelt," I said. Felice buckled up. I looked in the rearview mirror again, this time back at the road. It was still black and shining, with new cracks that left jagged gaps along its smooth endless line.

We made it back over the rutted road to the camp, saying very little, despite having just witnessed an unidentified earthshaking event. We decided it might have been a volcano, or it might have been an earthquake, but Felice held that either one was highly unlikely, given the thousands of years of geological quiet in the region.

"There would be some kind of warning," she insisted, fussing with the radio, which only crackled.

"Maybe this *is* the warning," I said, pulling up next to the picnic table and tent. We stuffed the sleeping bag and the blankets in the Pinto, and took down the tent in a hurry, to be on the safe side. I gathered up all of the trash and beer cans and Mickey's aluminum pan, which was blackened from the fire. Felice started to fill in the trench, so we could leave the place as we had found it, but I didn't think we had time for that. I took the shovel from her hand and slipped my arms around her inside her jacket. She leaned into me and stroked my hair. I turned my face to kiss her, but we were stiff-lipped and nervous, so we just held each other for a minute, then got into the Pinto and took the other fork down. I drove.

Felice didn't protest when I took the Pinto as fast as it would go around the steep curves. I slowed down when we got to the lower campsite. It was completely deserted, with no sign of all the kids and RVs that had been there the afternoon before.

"I guess everybody got off to an early start," I said. I looked at the dashboard clock. It was still before noon.

"Maybe they felt the tremor and got out of here faster than us," said Felice.

Finally, we came to a sign that said, "Leaving Mt. Estrella State Park. Come Again." It had said, "Entering Mt. Estrella State Park. Welcome" on the other side. There was a chain pulled across the road that hadn't been there when we'd come in. A rusty metal sign hung from it that said, "Closed for the Season," which seemed odd in August. Felice got out of the car and unhooked the chain from the post of the Come Again/Welcome sign so I could drive through, then refastened it and got back into the Pinto, saying, "This is creepy."

She started messing with the radio again. She found a light rock, a hard rock, and a talk station where the topic was mean family fights over wills, but there was no mention of any kind of geological occurrence, not even when the light rock station took a newsbreak to talk about the indictment against the governor's press secretary. We drove for what seemed like forever before we passed a couple of low-slung houses with laundry on the line and a car in the drive. We saw a farmer on a tractor circling a field, and he gave us a wave. We waved back and started giggling out of pure silly relief to see another person, even if he was mounted on a big machine several low barbed wire fences away from us.

A few miles farther on, we ran into a roadblock. The army men were all set up with signs and barricades and jeeps and sunglasses and a couple of big trucks parked off to the side of the road. We spotted them from a long way off, and I told Felice to hide the pot. She said she had no idea where it was, so I had to settle for lost instead of hidden. I also wanted her to be sure that the top of the trash bag was folded over so that they couldn't look inside and see the empty beer cans and peppermint schnapps bottle, but Felice refused to do a lot of turning around in the seat and rummaging. We approached the roadblock with something less than the warm, peacetime smile that the guy gave me as he motioned me to pull over.

He leaned on the door of the car as I rolled down the window. "Hi," he said, motioning his chin toward the mound of stuff in the back seat. "Been camping?"

"Yes, sir," I answered, hoping Felice wouldn't snicker.

The soldier nodded his big red chin and his sunglasses at me, and asked, "Where?"

"Mt. Estrella," said Felice, warming up a smile of her own. "Why, what's happening?"

The soldier didn't warm, and he didn't cool. He just beckoned his buddy over and asked, "Were you aware that the campground was closed?"

I was surprised that *he* was aware of it. "It was open when we got there yesterday afternoon, sir, but we saw the sign when we left this morning."

The buddy bent down behind the first guy and listened. Red Chin leaned closer to my face. "And you weren't informed that the campground was closing?" The buddy had pulled out a clipboard and was checking a list.

"No girls in a Pinto listed," he said.

"We were camping by ourselves," said Felice. "Up near the top. Nobody told us anything."

Red Chin asked for my license and Felice's ID, while the buddy walked around the Pinto and made a note of the plate number. We sat and waited while Red Chin went over to confer with a group of men sitting in the shade of one of the big trucks, and waited some more while he got into the cab of the truck and talked on a two-way radio. That was when I noticed that most of the jeeps and trucks were parked in a side road, next to an "Off Limits" sign that had a permanent look to it. I looked past the line of guys and barricades and vehicles, my eyes following the road a long distance, and I noticed how very black and shiny and new-looking it was. I nudged Felice. She got annoyed and said, "What?" just as Red Chin returned.

He reactivated his peace-time smile and handed us back our licenses. "Well, that's all fine. I hope you girls didn't have any trouble last night. Did the cold keep you up?"

I turned the key and started the engine. "We slept just fine."

He kept his hand on the door. "Strange weather we're having. There was a lot of thunder this morning. Hear it?"

I hoped he wouldn't notice that Felice had slipped her hand onto my seat so that it rested against the side of my leg as she answered, "We slept in late. We didn't hear a thing."

He nodded and stepped back, saying, "You girls go on home now. Drive careful."

We waved goodbye, and I left my window down as we drove off. "See that road out there?" I asked Felice. "Isn't that just like the one where you were running?"

She squinted her eyes, then moved her hand full onto my thigh as she nodded yes. We'd already decided that the tremor must have been some sort of army thing when the helicopters buzzed by.

THE DAY WAS almost gone by the time we got back to Mickey's house. Mickey was watching a baseball game on TV. Kenny was building a structure of toothpicks and Elmer's glue on a record cover at her feet. Toothpicks were scattered everywhere.

I dropped an armful of blankets onto a chair. "What are you making, Kenny?" I figured he owed me some small talk to make up for kicking a wading pool at my head.

He joined two intricate wooden webs with a precise white spot of glue. He didn't look up. "A sports super-dome."

"Don't mind him," said Mickey. "He's been playing soccer all day, and he's exhausted."

Felice brought in an armload of stuff to go back to the kitchen. "Mickey," she said, "we were bombed."

I was surprised that we were going to tell Mickey about it, but as long as we were, I wanted to get the facts straight.

"The ground shook. The army had a roadblock. *Maybe* it was a bomb."

Mickey glanced back at the TV screen as somebody got a hit. "Oh, where did you go? Mt. Estrella?"

She knew all about it. The army did tests out there that were supposed to be secret, but Mickey had talked to a guy she'd met in line at the bank. He was stationed at Fort Estrella and had money to burn. According to him, they were setting off bombs underground.

I saw the muscles in Felice's face tighten when Mickey said that. I think it was the idea of hidden miner-als being blasted to powder that upset her the most. She dumped the blankets off the chair onto the floor and stomped into the kitchen. She rattled some dishes in there, stomped out again, and started picking up the blankets and folding them into perfect squares.

Mickey patted the cushion of the couch, inviting me to sit down beside her. I noticed that her red nail polish looked a little chewed. We decided later that Mickey was lonely, because once she started talking, it was as if she couldn't stop.

I sat there trying to return to reality, watching Felice subdue the blankets, while Mickey turned down the sound on the game and told us how Felice's mother—Mickey called her Ida—used to take them ice skating when Felice was four and Mickey was almost fourteen. "Most of the mothers who came to the rink didn't skate. They sat in the warming house drinking awful coffee from styrofoam cups. But Ida got herself out on the ice," she said.

Kenny's breathing rose behind Mickey's voice. He had fallen asleep on the floor. Mickey bent to cover him with the afghan from the back of the couch. A faint whiff of potato chips floated up from his open mouth.

"It was something to see," Mickey said to Felice. "Ida would take your hand and skate out to dead center where the figure skaters worked on their jumps. She would arrange her scarf into a circle on the ice, then lift you into the middle of it and let you dance. You were cute, all eyes and red wool, sliding on your double runners and laughing. Ida would skate around the small circle of her scarf, waving her hands and wiggling with you, and even the fancy skaters would stop glaring for the pure joy you had in each other. The two of you had eyes for nobody else, so I got to do whatever I wanted most of the time."

Mickey looked at Felice, who was shaking out the sleeping bag. Her arms were making swift, sharp motions in the air and her face was shining in the light from the TV.

"You remind me of your mother," Mickey said.

Felice raised one eyebrow and scowled. She thrummed her fingers against the wood of the coffee table. Her nails made a loud clicking sound.

"I have no idea what you're talking about," she told Mickey.

Mickey and I laughed from the couch. It was a good impersonation.

Felice went back to folding blankets and Mickey kept talking. I couldn't concentrate on her story because every move Felice made seemed to gather all of the light in the room to her, and watching the lines of her arms made me shiver. While Mickey told about being good at the grapevine, her legs going in and out, in and out, leaving a pattern on the ice like hourglasses stacked one on top of the other, I could feel Felice's warm weight on me again. I watched Felice put a stack of blankets on the shelf, her hands disappearing in the folds of wool and nylon. Mickey remembered the boys in their smooth black skates, taking the corners hockey style. I tried to imagine what it meant that Felice and her mother had looked at each other with joy in their eyes.

Mickey touched my elbow for attention. "One time I sat with the guy who ran the popcorn machine in his silver Plymouth. Ida came looking for me on her bare blades on the asphalt, and when she found me with his hand in my shirt, she hauled off and started kicking his tires as hard as she could with her skate."

Felice, her arms still in the linen closet, rolled her eyes, but it wasn't funny. Mickey reached out with her foot and rubbed sleeping Kenny's back with her toes. "I took off running and hitchhiked home. I felt bad later that I hadn't taken you with me, Felice, because when Ida got that mad, she spread it around."

Felice said, "I don't remember any of that."

Mickey took a long drag on her cigarette. "Ida didn't speak to me for months." She got up from the couch and bent to shake Kenny's shoulder. He mumbled and stood without seeming to wake up. His eyes were barely open, and he had toothpicks in his hair. Mickey brushed them off, and said, "It was a hundred years ago." She took Kenny's hand and led him upstairs to go to bed.

Felice pulled me up off the couch. "We should do something," she said.

I felt dread—please, god, not a disco. "I don't have any money left," I told her.

She slid open the door to the patio. "Let's go outside."

We sat on the grass. The big moon gave me shadows to watch. Felice was restless. My eye caught on the line of her shin, sharp and shining in the dark. I touched her hand, and she let me, but when I bent to kiss her, she said, "Not here," jerking her head back toward the house. I looked up, and sure enough, there was Kenny's tow head peeping over the sill of a second story window with an Incredible Hulk decal on the glass.

Felice leaned and whispered to me again about Mickey's wet-rimmed glass that she pressed to bedroom walls. I didn't think Mickey was as interested in us as she was in Rick's private phone calls, but Felice was not persuaded. She rubbed her heels back and forth in the grass until she had cleared two small round pits down to dirt. I rolled onto my back and gazed at the moon. It was waning, but I still felt intensity in the light. Felice started bombarding me with bits of grass. I sat up.

"Stop it," I said. "I'm allergic."

Felice threw a whole handful of grass into the air. It looked to me as if she were aiming at the moon. Most of it fell back in her face. She shook it off.

"We should do something," she said again.

I blew a piece of grass off her cheek. "Like what?"

"Sabotage," she said. "Defuse the bombs."

I flopped back down on the ground again. "We're not going to do that."

She crossed her arms tightly on her chest. I could see that she was serious. "Why not?"

I had plenty of reasons. "Because they have guns. Besides, it's too far away, and we would have no idea what to do. And I'd be too scared."

I looked at Felice's moonshadow nodding her head. "All right," she said, "something close." I snorted. She put her warm hand on my head. Her shadow arm looked like a stem that connected her to me.

We decided to target a neighborhood cop. Felice didn't have anything against this particular guy, except that he looked at her hard when she ran on the highway, but he was as close as I was willing to go to the armed forces. As it was, I was miserable while we talked about it. I was even more miserable once we were walking to the street where Felice knew he lived, with a bag full of ornamental gravel we had scooped up from around the neighbor's bushes. It wasn't much past ten o'clock, but no one was out on the streets. We walked past a yard where the sprinkler was going, and I nudged Felice.

"Remember sneaking into Mrs. Peterson's garden to eat the morning-glories?"

Felice nodded, intent on the job at hand. "We were young," she said.

We left the sound of the sprinkler behind and turned a corner into another silent street. I could see the outline of the squad car in the moonlight. Jeff had a Matchbox car just like it when he was a kid, down to the little red light on the top. We stood on the corner, peering at the house where the squad car was parked. My hands were shaking. "I can't believe I'm about to become a vandal," I whispered.

"One light on," Felice said. "Probably the bedroom. Let's go." She walked calmly down the sidewalk toward the car, swinging the bag of gravel a little as she moved. I tried to match her pace, increasingly overwhelmed with the worry that neighbors glancing out of their windows would be able to identify me later by my fat silhouette. And I'd never be able to run as fast as Felice to get away. She didn't really need my help, so what was I doing here? We stopped beside the hedge bordering the cop's yard and squatted down, shielded from the window. Felice shifted the gravel into one corner to use as a spout. The crackle of the brown paper sounded like gunshot to me. She gave my hand a squeeze. "Keep watch," she whispered. She crossed the driveway in the beam from the window, then knelt in the shadow of the car. I saw her open the gas tank and raise the bag to pour the gravel into the tank. It made a strange, soft sound, like rice being poured into a pot to boil.

I was getting fuller and fuller where I crouched, too, fighting queasiness and excitement, until I had to stand up to give the feelings more room. I must have rustled the bushes, because a dog in the cop's house started barking. Felice pulled the bag to her chest and froze there, kneeling next to the rear tire. A hall light went on, and the front door swung open. I heard the thud as a big, black labrador threw himself at the screen door. A woman in a velvety red bathrobe stood behind the screen, looking out across the yard. The dog bared his teeth, barking loud enough to wake the neighbors. The woman put her hand on his head, talking softly. She gave the yard one last look before shutting the door. I thought that my mother would probably like her. I hadn't dared look at Felice while the door was open, but she was stock-still in the same kneeling position. She didn't move until the light went out in the hall, then she reached for the handle of the passenger door which opened miraculously, just like the ones on Jeff's Matchbox car, except this one gave a loud creak. I was horrified—what was she doing now? She ducked her head into the car for a moment, then scrambled back to the hedge, keeping well below the line of sight from the window. She stood beside me, breathing hard. When we looked at each other, I knew we had to get moving, because I could barely control my sudden desire to laugh.

We didn't run until we were out of sight of the house. I caught up with Felice when she stopped to dump the rest of the white gravel at the bush where we'd gotten it. She waited until we were safely in her bedroom before she reached into the pocket of her shorts to show me the pair of mirrored sunglasses she'd stolen off the dash.

She put them on and gave me her best Clint Eastwood profile. "The revenge of the earth," she muttered.

I laughed until she hissed, "Shhhhh. Mickey." I couldn't come down from the tension, but Felice was ready to crash. I lay in her bed with my heart pounding, holding the edge of her pillowcase, feeling both freed and caught. She had been breathing even and slow for a long time when she reached back and pulled my arm around her, so that when I finally slept, I was holding her close.

FELICE HAD TO be at work by eleven, and we woke up at ten-thirty, so she was in a rush. There was no time for talk. She turned Donna Summer up loud on the stereo and went to take a shower.

I shook the pine needles out of my shorts, pulled a clean t-shirt and some muddy socks out of my backpack, and I was ready to go. I made the bed, guestlike, and carried my pack into the living room. Kenny was watching cartoons and eating Quisp.

I spoke to the back of his soccer team shirt. "Where's your mom?"

"Work," he answered, still staring at Scooby-Doo.

I went to the kitchen to help myself to another pair of Pop Tarts. While they were in the toaster, I looked at the pudgy picture of Felice on the refrigerator door. It made me nervous, so I kissed my finger and touched her little film face. That didn't settle me much. I opened the door and got out some milk.

I went back to the bedroom after I'd eaten. Felice had pulled her hair into a tight bun, but tendrils were escaping over her forehead already. She was tugging a skimpy black top with spaghetti straps over her head.

I leaned on the door frame. "You get to wear that to work?"

She started throwing clothes around, looking for her purse. "I wear whatever I want. I work in the back."

She found the purse and took a step toward me and the door. I touched her arm. Suddenly, Kenny pushed around me and landed a kick in a pile of clothes on the floor. "You're such a slob," he said.

Felice put her palm around his blond head and pushed him all the way back into the living room. She slung her purse over her shoulder, looking at me. "I've got to go," she said.

We stepped out into sunlight that hazed our eyes, it was so bright. I blinked to get my sight back, and the first thing I saw was a couple of little girls in the yard next door. They were scooping dust into red plastic tea cups and offering the cups to each other.

"Why, *thank you*, Missy, for the wonderful tea," said the one with a frog on her sweatshirt.

"You're welcome, Missy," said the other one, "thank *you.*" They dumped the dirt all over each other's laps.

Felice fished her big quartz key chain out of her purse. That was a shock. I had been assuming that I was going to drive her to work. I heard a rattle and turned around. Kenny was pressing his nose against the front door screen, so it looked broad and flat and white. The little girls saw him, too, and elaborately got up and moved all of their stuff, sitting down again with their backs toward him. I glanced back at Kenny. He seemed implacable, and his tongue had joined his nose flat against the screen. "Bye," I said to him.

His face sort of wagged. I thought it was a nod. Felice added, "Stay out of my bedroom."

Kenny disappeared. The little girls were busily stuffing a red teapot with handfuls of dry grass that they pulled out of the lawn with great effort. "You driving?" I asked Felice.

"Of course, that's how I always get to work." She took a step toward the white Valiant at the curb.

"Whose car?" I stood my ground. We were sharing the sidewalk, about two feet apart.

Felice took another step, splaying the keys on her ring and sticking one between each of her fingers, as we'd been told to do in Health for self-defense. "It's Mickey's, but she lets me use it. She carpools."

From the sky, something fell between us on the hot sidewalk. Splat. It was a water balloon. Kenny's head was sticking out of a second-story window with filmy pink curtains. The bathroom. "Creep!" yelled Felice.

The little girls looked up, tense and expectant. They knew the next balloon would be meant for them. "Let's get out of here," said Felice. The little girls were gathering rocks in their cups. I could hear water running from the faucet in the bathroom. Felice and I ran for our cars.

I followed her when she pulled out. We hadn't really said goodbye. I wished we had CBs, so I could radio over and make sure that it was okay for me to drive with her to the restaurant.

She drove slowly through the broad streets. I was distracted, staring at yucca blooming in the yards, not really paying attention to where I was going. She took a right, and my stomach clenched, because we were driving past the cop's house. The patrol car was still sitting there, looking flawless and inviolable, but it hadn't moved. Felice beeped her horn and gave me a thumbs up.

My heart hit my forehead. I wasn't cut out for life on the wrong side of the law. I pulled onto the left side of the road and passed Felice, flooring it into the first side street, just to get away from the scene of the crime. I had to make a U-turn and skulk at the corner, waiting for Felice so I'd know where to go. It was a short wait, but of course I had to pull out behind her back onto the street I'd just escaped. Felice shook her head at me, a few more tendrils of hair falling onto her neck. I kept my eyes on her the rest of the way to the restaurant, watching the slight shifts of her shoulders and the little flashes of white as her hands slid in and out of my line of vision on the steering wheel. I tried to see her as clearly as I could, so I could miss a true picture of her, but it was hard to make her out through all that window glass.

When we got to the cafe, Felice pulled around back and I followed. She parked next to a big, black, shiny pickup with a Grateful Dead decal in the window. There wasn't a space for the Pinto, so I stayed in the car. Felice jumped out and ran back to me, her purse swinging from her shoulder. She leaned into the Pinto's open window.

"I'm glad you came," she said.

Her mascara had globbed up, leaving a small blue lump in the corner of her eye. I dabbed it away with my fingertip. She didn't blink. "This is hard," I said.

She nodded. Her lip trembled and her cheeks swelled up. She looked a lot more like herself at ten than a woman with a job she'd better not be late to. She pushed the wisps of hair from her bun back behind her ears and put her hand on my neck. My skin got hot where she was touching me.

"I'm going to miss you, Char."

I leaned my face against her hand. "Just until school starts. It's only a couple more weeks."

She started to cry. I reached up and hugged her as best I could, pressing against the inside of the door. Our foreheads touched, then she kissed me. I heard the back door of the cafe open. Felice pulled away.

"Bye," she whispered. "Stay out of jail."

Even this early in the day, heat was pumping out from the kitchen through the open door. A tall, hairy-armed guy came out, holding a plastic trash bag. It had to be Tony.

He was looking right at us, but nothing on his face marked that he'd seen us kissing. He didn't seem to see me at all. To tell the truth, I didn't get him into such great focus, either. Mostly I saw the trash bag, which was gold-colored and bulging. He tossed it into the dumpster and gave a twisty whistle through his teeth at Felice.

She walked into the kitchen without glancing his way. He reached out and tugged at her bun as she passed. He must have pulled pretty hard, because half of it unwrapped and fell down her neck. I expected Felice to turn around and slug him, but she just disappeared through the door. He followed, then I heard her laugh.

I switched the radio on and backed out. It took me the best part of an hour to find the on-ramp to the highway. I was so tired on the drive home that I barely saw the view. I just drove, hot, straight, flat out. My mind was numb, but my body was thinking. I'd reach to signal a lane change, and all along my arm, the skin would be remembering her hand on it, light and warm. As I was driving over the pass, the fir trees shook, and for an instant I was afraid for the ground beneath me. I thought I felt it crumbling away beneath the road, but it was only the wind.

Chapter Fourteen

MY FIRST DAY BACK AT WORK AFTER THE LONG weekend, I knew that the nursing home was not where I wanted to be. Smells hit me as soon as I walked in the front door: ammonia and stale, overburdened air. My uniform made me sweat and itch more than ever. It reminded me of the spookhouse at the amusement park Felice and I had gone to at least twenty times last summer; the jolts were too familiar to be exciting. I didn't want the vague smiles I got from the women in their chairs in the hall. I told myself that they smiled that way at everyone. The halls seemed quite a bit sparser than usual. I stopped Kiley, who was wheeling a cart of bed linen from room to room, and asked her where everyone was.

"Oh, there's one of those Girl Scout sing-alongs in the cafeteria," she said. "Your whole wing was rounded up for it."

I went to the door of the wing and peered through the little window. All I saw was a nurse I didn't know signing things at the nurse's station. I stood a moment at the window, watching nothing happening, then I bent down to get my key on its neckchain into the lock.

I checked in with the nurse, and she told me to go on over to the cafeteria to help wheel folks back from the sing-along. As I walked down the long, nearly empty hall, I heard the echoes of my soft-soled shoes and the voices coming from behind the cafeteria double doors. The singing seemed like a loud noise being muffled, so I was surprised when I pushed through the doors, because they really weren't making much sound at all. The room was packed, with tables full of women in loose dresses and buttondown sweaters, and wheelchairs wedged in between the tables and lined up along the walls. Most of the aides were gathered near the kitchen doors. Some of them were actually in the kitchen, talking and semi-sneaking a smoke. I gave them a wave and went to lean on the back of Mabel's chair. I saw Ginny, but I avoided her eye. I didn't feel like talking to anybody, and Ginny might ask how my trip was. I didn't see Peg at all, but that was no surprise. She didn't sing, especially not hymns.

There were only nine or ten Girl Scouts, and none of them seemed to have much of a bent for music. They were wrapping up "Onward Christian Soldiers" with the help of a few willing women close to the front, but they seemed about to drop the cross of Jesus as they struggled with the last few notes. The leader must have decided to go ahead and let it drop, because after smiling over her shoulder to acknowledge the spattering of applause, she whispered something to the girls, raised her arms, and they dove into a popular song of fifty or sixty years ago:

Come away with me, Lucile
In my merry Oldsmobile

They did okay with the first couple of lines, in a ragged, child-choir way, but when they got to the third line, Iris started to sing. She was near the back of the room, tied into her chair, and her voice was loud and high.

Down the road of life we'll fly
Automobubbling, you and I

The girls must have found Iris a little scary, because their voices faded away almost entirely. It didn't matter, though, because Iris had found the pitch and was going strong.

To the church we'll swiftly steal

Mabel started to sing, too; so did Ed. I looked at Ginny again. She wasn't singing—the song wasn't from a time of hers—but she was swaying a little, listening.

Then our wedding bells will peal

The women at the tables in front who had been going at it with the hymns opened up again, and their momentum carried the song into a repetition of the chorus. Nobody seemed to know a verse. If the Girl Scouts had practiced one, they weren't about to impose it at this point.
You can go as far as you like with me
In my merry Oldsmobile.

I was floating on the voices, seeing Iris in her thirties, waltzing through a Washington party. All the diplomats were letting their hair down, and Iris was laughing and making faces over her partner's shoulder to her friend with the violet eyes in the crowd, but suddenly my mind stopped floating on the imagined past and settled into my head, at home. I had been coming into my body all summer, and as I leaned there listening, I arrived.

I felt warm, as if I were starting to glow. I was very aware of myself, as usual—aware of being young, of being fat, of having the use of my legs and hands, but for once I didn't have to slip those useful hands secretly under the elastic of my white uniform pants to feel my belly and confirm what size it was. I knew it from the inside, because all of a sudden I seemed to go out to the edge of my skin.

It was weird. My arm brushed against the leather of Mabel's chair, and I prickled. The hair in each pore stood on end. I felt goosebumps rising all up my legs, on my back, on my scalp, too. I was vibrating, as if the air around me were tracing my form so I could locate myself exactly, as if my blood were doing the same thing inside. I could feel my muscles pulling against each other to hold me to my bones. I felt my stretching lungs, and my uterus tucked in me like a fist in a glove. I completely understood what kind of animal I was.

Just when the feeling was becoming so intense as to be painful, I saw the cafeteria walls start to throb. The song was still going, and most everyone was singing. I'd lost the words into a crackling liquid sound that didn't seem to have much to do with the motion of their mouths. Everyone looked bright, lit from within. The gray-skinned people were shining gray, and the folks who weren't singing were moving their eyes or had their lids folded down as if to sleep. We were all separate, but as much as we contained ourselves, we spilled out, too, out into the air and the song and the walls.

"My god," I thought, "this is only a summer job."

Most of the Girl Scouts had degenerated into giggling behind their hands and pointing, except for one little pink-cheeked blonde who was still singing as loud as she could, way off key. I figured she had to be the scout leader's daughter. The leader's eyes were dewy with tears when the song was finally done, and she gave her little blonde a hug, leading her out by the hand to talk with some of the folks. I had to get out of there. I flipped the locks off the wheels of Mabel's chair and backed her up.

"Just a minute," she was saying, "just a minute."

I felt mean, but I had to stop and ask her what the problem was.

"I don't know," she said, irritated. "Just a minute."

"I haven't got all day, Mabel. You want to talk to the kids, is that it?" I was confused at the sound of my voice, which was coarse and irritated when I felt transformed.

Mabel looked at her hands for a moment, then back at me, her eyes a startling blue. "Just a minute," she said with cold fury, so I locked her wheels again and left her sitting there until she was almost the last.

The other folks settled back into their ordinary selves, decently separate from me, but I stayed aware of Mabel and myself as intensely connected and alive. Every time I looked over at her glaring at me from her chair, it gave me a jolt, so I had to make her wait.

After I finally left Mabel next to her bed, I went out to the main lobby and leaned on the wall. I knew it wouldn't look right for an aide to be sitting in one of the big padded chairs they kept out there for show. I didn't stay very long anyway, but stood up, tugging on the hem of my tunic. I walked back through the lobby and down the hall to the business offices, where I knocked on the bald man's door and gave my two week's notice.

He nodded and looked mildly distressed, and asked me my name again.

School was starting in three weeks. It had been my plan all along to quit in the fall. This had been nothing but a temporary thing, like Felice washing dishes. I was finished with it. I told myself there wasn't anything weird in the way I was ducking out.

That was the last day I paid attention to my job. For the next two weeks, I was practically sleep-working. I was happy when I walked into the nursing home. I was humming. The lawn had been cured into a brown mat by the August sun, and I secretly believed that I had sucked all of its green into me; I had that much tart juice.

Mom and I went to some shops to pick out a couple of cute outfits for school. I had trouble finding things that fit, but it didn't matter. I ended up with some tunics with elastic in the sleeves and big flowers all over them. I imagined blooming in the halls at school, dripping daisies down my back, morning-glories filling my arms, a black iris at each ear. Felice and I would be a complete eco-system—nobody would have to water us. And all of the pretty girls in their autumn colors, in their black and gold cheerleader skirts, in their wine sweaters and crimson slacks, they could imitate fall leaves and fire until their pure skins grew shiny with sweat and effort, and their boyfriends had to bring each of them a diet Coke to keep them clogged and cool. I couldn't care less what they did.

The days passed fast. I didn't tell anyone I was leaving, but some of the aides caught on. Perez said something to me about making my escape, but I just looked at her. I didn't want any kind of goodbye. Mostly, I didn't think about leaving the nursing home at all. I just put it out of my mind. But my body knew. My step got brisker. My hands, which used to reach to change the padding on a bed as if they were moving through pudding, now cut the air sharply; there was so much less between them and the task to be done. I changed beds with scarcely a thought for their corners, yet they were unwrinkled and firmly tucked.

I spoke cheerily to Ginny and Peg, but I didn't look into their eyes, didn't follow their glances to read them, like I used to. I avoided Peg as much as I could, because I was walking around wrapped in a rich, dreamy feeling I called Felice, and my dream Felice got pierced by Peg's one clear eye and glanced over by her clouded, sliding one. It was uncomfortable.

Peg and Ginny were caught up in their own projects anyway. Peg was getting letters almost every day, and they were following up on Ginny's application for public housing, so they mostly just asked me to Xerox forms for them and put stamps on envelopes. That was fine with me. I didn't want Peg to penetrate my dream cloud any more than she did just by looking at me, but there was another pressure in me, pushing me to talk. Some nights, I would get a little wild wanting to get Peg alone in the TV room and ask her what she knew about the love of women and patience, and if there were certain things that were important to say, and could two girls go out in high school, and did she think we'd ruin our friendship? I wanted to know for sure if Peg was risking everything with Ginny, if they really did meet each other straight on with their bodies and their hearts, or if I was just looking at them funny because I was funny. Was such a thing even possible? I knew it couldn't happen completely, here in the nursing home, where everyone who bothered with any kind of alertness knew the intimate habits of everyone else, and the rules didn't allow a closed door.

I never found Peg alone when the questioning mood was on me, so I slipped through the days dreaming Felice. Earlier in the summer, I'd been clearing off the passenger seat in the Pinto for her every time I got into the car. Now I didn't have to bother, because she was already sitting down with me, inside me. I'd be cutting meat for Mabel and feeling the way Felice had reached her arm around me and held me while we slept. It seemed to make me safe. Or I'd be trying to give Iris a sponge bath, and I'd be hearing Felice talking, tenderly telling me the names of rocks, or I'd see her hand flicking the radio dial. I'd give Shelley a sip of juice, and Felice would be kissing me through the open car window again.

All of this daydreaming kept me calm as I went about my work. As the days went by, though, a furtive excitement began to nag at me, and rattle my composure. I began to look forward to leaving the nursing home. I wanted out. It built in me like a secret. It *was* a secret. Just ten working days, then nine, then five. On my last day, I let Mrs. Eugenia Cribbs introduce me to the niceties of using clips to make waves in her hair after a shampoo, a thing she trusted only to veteran aides. I knew that next week she would have to show someone else, but I never said a word. After my session with her, feeling a little uneasy, I slipped into Mr. Pierson's room.

Mr. Pierson's health had been failing. He didn't sit up at all now but stayed stiffly curled in his bed, and his skin was losing its pink. Someone had left "Dialing for Dollars" on the TV in front of him. The host was letting his studio phone ring, trying to give away the cash jackpot. I leaned over the bed, and said, "Mr. Pierson, I'm leaving."

He didn't stir. I stared at his thin, thin shoulders, watching for any motion in the TV light. Nothing.

"I won't be coming back," I told him. I pulled down the blanket and watched his chest. He had a white under-shirt on. I squatted down so I could look across him horizontally, and I could see the sign of his breath that way, a slight rise and fall, but enough to let me finish my goodbye as if this was the only one that mattered.

I pulled his blanket back up and tucked it in around him. I rested my hand on his cheek a moment. It was dry and papery, although the air in the room felt damp.

"Sweet dreams." I turned off the TV set as I left.

I was already in the parking lot, putting my key into the door of the Pinto, when I heard my name. I swung around. Peg was sitting at the edge of the curb in her chair. The sidewalk to the staff parking lot didn't have any curb cuts, so that was as far as she could go. Her black hair was loose around her shoulders. She said my name again. "Char." I had a feeling that she'd be shouting if she could.

I walked back over to her, still holding the key. "Peg?"

Her mouth had small spots of white around it, as if she was straining her muscles to say, or not say, some-thing. She hit reverse on her chair, pulling back a few paces from the curb. I put my foot up on it and leaned on my knee, trying to look relaxed.

"You're leaving," she said.

For a wild moment, I imagined that Mr. Pierson had told her. I nodded, caught in the act. "Yeah, this is my last day."

"You didn't tell me." She was looking straight at me, but her left eye kept sliding sideways, then jerking back.

I traced the edge of my car key with my thumbnail, trying to think of something to say. I shrugged and lied, "I didn't tell anyone."

Peg stared at that shrug like it was an old horror movie that still gave her the creeps. "You didn't even bother to say goodbye. Maybe it didn't occur to you."

I let the key ring dangle from my little finger. "Peg, I didn't mean to hurt your feelings. School's about to start."

She snorted. "Well, you'd better go study, then."

We stayed there at the edge of the curb looking at each other for another minute. I think my eyes, both of them, started to slide around before either of hers budged. I looked at her red hands curled in her lap and lied again, "I don't know what I did to make you so mad."

She raised one of her hands and shook it in my face. "You don't have the first idea of how to be a friend." Her arm dropped back in her lap, and I could tell she was done. "You're a kid," she said. "Go on home."

I did.

Chapter
Fifteen

I FELT BAD ABOUT PEG, BUT I LET HER SLIP from my mind. I wasn't thinking about anything except Felice and the start of school. On the first day of classes, I got Mom to put my hair into a bun, and I wore one of my new flower shirts. She shed a few tears over how grown-up I looked. I told her not to pack me a lunch.

I drove the Pinto and got to school early. The halls were nearly empty, the floors gleamed. For a moment I expected to smell ammonia, as if I were back at the nursing home. I was hugging a heavy grocery sack under one arm, holding up my schedule, and trying to find the number of the locker Felice and I were going to share. Seniors were allowed to pick their partners.

When I finally found the right number, the girl in the locker next to us was already there. Her name was Beverly. I'd known her for years. They used to call her Beaver because of her teeth, and she cheated at tetherball by grabbing the rope. She had streaked her hair over the summer and made the pompom squad. "Hi," she said to me, in uniform.

"Hi." I hoped she'd be gone before Felice showed up. I was a little disappointed that Felice wasn't waiting for me here, but it gave me time to decorate the locker.

Beverly was hanging up a picture of Sylvester Stallone as Rocky, in boxing trunks, all glistening with sweat. She taped it neatly to the inside of the locker door, and glanced over to see what I was doing. I was unrolling an equally glossy picture of a volcano, overflowing with red hot lava. My picture was too big to fit inside the door. Beverly loaned me her scissors so I could trim the edges.

"I guess you're into nature," she said, picking at a rough spot in her nail polish with the tip of her pen.

Beverly spotted another clump of pompoms across the hall, and they walked off in the direction of the cafeteria, practicing a cheer half under their breaths. I waited until they were out of sight before I opened the paper bag and scooped out handfuls of rocks. I'd brought every single one that Felice had sent me over the summer. They completely filled the second shelf. I left the top shelf for Felice's books, and figured that I could use the space at the bottom of the locker, if we wanted to leave the rocks on the other shelf for a while. I arranged the small shiny ones in front and the big monumental ones behind. They looked impressive. When I picked one up, I could almost feel a heartbeat in my hand.

I shut the door so Felice would get the full effect when she got there. Felice was almost never on time, but I'd hoped that we'd have a chance to say hi or something before the first class. I'd sent her a couple of careful letters, with just "love, Char" at the bottom, but I hadn't heard from her at all. A river of kids was flowing past me now, and I tossed out a few good-to-see-yous. I noticed that none of the other girls had flowers on their shirts. The hall was filled with solid sweaters and tweed jackets with elbow patches, but that didn't matter. Where was Felice? I got the big-toothed comb out of my backpack and worked on my bangs.

The warning bell rang. I gave up. I knew I would see her fifth period because we were both taking a seniors-only geology class. It had an overnight field trip to the Garden of the Gods in the spring.

The periods were short since this was a half day. The teachers looked odd to me, excessively human, even though all they were doing was passing out books and assigning seats. My English teacher's slip was showing, and there were tears in her eyes already, on the first day of school. I went back to the locker between every class, but there was no sign of Felice. She didn't show up for geology, either. I decided she must be getting back from New Mexico a day or two late. Mr. Coolig, the geology teacher, wore a baggy green jacket with pockets full of nuts, which he ate in class. He was the only teacher who went ahead and introduced a few concepts.

"Uniformitarianism is the belief that the present is the key to the past. This is different from what people used to believe were great catastrophes followed by the sudden creation of new types of life." He cracked a peanut between his teeth, slipping the empty shell back into his pocket. I'd heard that he sometimes threw the shells at kids who were talking or sleeping in his class. I really tried to listen, so I could catch Felice up on what she missed, but I got lost somewhere between the Great Flood and the Scientific Method.

I saw Beverly at the locker again at the end of the day. I didn't need to get anything out or leave anything there, but I opened it one more time, just to be sure that Felice hadn't left a note. Beverly stared at the shelf full of rocks, but she didn't comment. Instead she said, "Where's Felice Ventura this year? You're friends with her, aren't you?"

I figured Beverly was just pruning her social skills, because she was paying a lot more attention to spreading lotion on her legs than to me trying to come up with an answer.

"I don't know. She must be around somewhere. I saw her this summer." I watched Beverly bending over with her back to her locker, massaging her calves with her palms. Rocky looked tough but vulnerable behind her. "Why?"

Beverly had reached her ankles, and she was circling them with her fingertips. She looked up at me. "She hasn't moved, has she? You want some of this?" She offered me the pink purse-sized bottle of Jergens.

I got a shiver. "No," I said. "No, thanks. She hasn't moved. I don't want any lotion." I shut my locker with a polite little click, turned, and walked away. I thought if I didn't find out what was happening with Felice within the next five minutes, my brain was going to burst. And I was scared that I had been staring too hard at Beverly's legs, a possibility that filled me with dread. I decided to call Felice from the pay phone in the basement and put myself out of my misery.

I walked down the concrete steps to the basement. The school had been built on the site of an old landfill, so the foundations were shifting as the garbage beneath them shifted, and the walls in the basement were cracking. I went into the girls' locker room where the phone was. The swim team was getting ready to practice, pulling on suits and throwing soap at each other. I dropped my dime and dialed Felice's number. I got a busy signal. A bar of soap came sliding across the floor to my feet. I gave it an awkward kick with the toe of my tennis shoe, then hunched over the booth to dial again. Busy. Felice *must* be back. She had stayed at home, sick or hung over. The swim team was in the showers in their suits. It was a rule: you had to rinse before you went into the pool. I always wondered exactly what was supposed to be washed away that chlorine couldn't kill. I tried again. Still busy. Felice wasn't hanging up the phone. The team took the door to the pool, shivering and giggling. I decided to drive by her house on my way home.

I hadn't counted on Mrs. Ventura being there, but her car was in the drive. Usually she was still at work this time of day. I didn't want to talk to her, but I couldn't tell if Felice was in the house or not. I went around to the backyard and peered in the sliding glass door. Mrs. Ventura was sitting at the kitchen table drinking coffee and dialing the phone. She would hold the receiver to her ear for a few seconds, then hang up and dial again. I knew just by watching her fingers that I had to get out of there. She looked up and saw me just as I was going round the corner of the house and came out to the back porch, calling, "Charlotte. Char. Come here." I pretended not to hear her and got into the Pinto. She didn't come to the front door, but I think she kept calling out the back, because as I pulled out I heard her shout something about Felice.

I was still upset when I pulled into the carport and found the letter in the mailbox. It said "F. Ventura" in the corner of the envelope, just as bold and fuschia as ever. I could see that it didn't have any kind of rock with it; it was just one sheet of paper. I stood there on the front step to read it. It said:

Dear Char:

I'm not coming back, not right away anyway. Mickey says I can stay here and take care of Kenny in the afternoons while she's at her job. I enrolled at this high school. It'll be good—I can establish residency for the state university. They've got a great geology department.

I can't live with my mother anymore, Char. It would be stupid for me to try, I just can't. Plus, there's this thing with Tony.

Write to me, all right? I'll be up there sometime, definitely for Christmas. Don't be mad, even though you've got a right to be. I hadn't decided yet when you were here, or I would have told you to your face.

They're not letting anyone near Mt. Estrella these days. Got the road completely blocked off. For construction, they say. I read it in the paper. The cop's got a new cruiser.

I miss you all the time, Char.

love,

Felice

I finished the letter, turned around, and got back into the Pinto. I didn't want to go inside and have Mom ask how my day had been.

I drove into the foothills. The pines were shifting in front of the unreal blue sky. At Tuckers Park I stopped and rested my head against the steering wheel. My stomach was heaving as if I'd been mixing vodka and cheap wine, but I hadn't had a drink since I'd seen Felice. Felice. I opened the door to breathe in the cool air. I could see Felice leaning out from a rock ledge above me, reaching to catch a piece of fool's gold, only this time she falls. I sobbed. I watched her body spinning and turning in the air. I barely managed to get out of the car so I could throw up a few feet away.

For a long time, I leaned against a tree as the air chilled. I didn't have any words or pictures in my head, just dead weight. The cracked bark left sap on my face. Dark was coming on.

The sour taste in my mouth reminded me I needed to take care of my mess. I covered the vomit with leaves and the coarsely ground rock that passed for dirt here. I scraped up one last fistful of rock and threw it as hard as I could at the Pinto, where it made pits and scratches in the paint.

I TOOK THE long way home, driving and crying. For a while I was lost in a suburb that looked just like Moody, but wasn't. It was after eleven by the time I pulled up in front of the house. A light was on in the living room.

Mom looked at me when I walked in the door. I knew Dad would have been in bed for at least an hour by now. Her eyes were red and puffy. A paperback novel was open in her lap. I recognized a spy book about a middle-aged woman who goes to work for the CIA. Mom had a cup of tea next to her on the arm of the couch. Her heart was in the cup. I could see it beating against the flo-thru tea bag. I squinted and waited for it to go back to being just Lipton. She took a sip.

"Where have you been?" She pulled the dripping tea bag out of her cup and set it on the saucer.

"I was at a late movie."

"Why didn't you call? You missed supper." Her stubby family fingers lay across the pages of the book.

"I tried to call, but it was busy, then the phone was out of order at the drive-in." I was too stupid-tired to talk with her. I could barely stand there, leaning unsteadily on the back of the couch, but I couldn't just walk past her to my room. Her velour robe had been zipped crooked, and her face was flushed. For an instant she reminded me of Peg. I sat down on the couch and tried to look my mother in the eye.

"I got a letter from Felice," I said. "She's not coming back."

"Oh, honey," said Mom, "that's too bad."

My arm was shaking as I leaned on the couch. She must have felt it. She glanced down at her book. I watched a motion pass through her face. It was like a picture in an anatomy book, where half of a woman's face is peeled back layer by layer to teach about the fat and cartilage and bone underneath. Something shifted in a lower layer. I saw folds like ripple marks around her mouth.

She looked back up at me, gazing steadily. It occurred to me that I'd assumed she'd been crying out of worry over me, but maybe something else was wrong. I didn't have any way to ask her.

"I saved you a pork chop," said Mom. She reached up and squeezed my hand where it rested on the couch. "Eat it if you're hungry, then go on to bed." She handed me her cup and saucer. "Take this into the kitchen for me, will you?"

I poured the cold tea into the sink, wondering what she hadn't said.

DAD LEFT FOR work before I got up in the morning, but he'd seen the scratched-up paint on the Pinto and taken my car keys away for a month. I was too numb to care. I rode the bus to school, wearing a loose gray jumper every day. Classes were fine. I sat there watching the teacher's mouth or looking at the roots of the hair of whoever was seated in front of me. It was easy to follow the waves of kids from class to class, but it was harder to know what time it was in the mornings and after school. Reading was difficult, but I was okay if there was some kind of worksheet or study question in front of me. I could just pull something off the page and write it down without having to interact with it much.

I never daydreamed anymore. I'd sit on the school lawn at lunchtime, rigid with misery, but I wasn't looking at anything inside my head. I'd look straight out at the small trees, the leaves, the dry brown grass, every stem and blade sharp and clear. This wasn't in single trans-fixed moments. It was constant. The focus of my life had changed. It had gone to details. I walked out in traffic, watching the yellow gray of the sky. The honking horns let me know there was a problem. I was best not moving, but it didn't really matter.

Felice had been my best friend for most of my school life. Other girls asked about her. She was fairly popular. I'd tell them that she'd moved to New Mexico. Every time I said that, I felt like I was wading in one of those intermit-tent streams I'd heard about in geology, the ones that only exist during spring snowmelt. They were commonly found in the arid or semiarid parts of the western United States. I had dumped all of the rocks from the locker back into another grocery bag and left them in a corner of my room.

Afternoons, I stayed in bed. Sometimes I'd sleep, but mostly I'd lie there watching the light from the window play over the plaster ceiling. I'd set my alarm clock for five and be up sitting in the living room in front of the television by the time Mom got home from work. I didn't want her to worry.

Sometimes in bed I would drift into a light sleep, which, like my waking life, was innocent of dreams. I think that was the state I was in when a bomb went off in my head. I saw the flash and heard a thundering in my ears, so I sat up. I didn't put my hand up to feel my skull. It didn't matter if it were in pieces or not. I whispered to myself to be calm, and soon enough, it stopped. I looked at the clock and saw that I had overslept. I could hear Mom getting supper ready. I glanced at my quilt to be sure that there were no bone fragments, then decided that I had to do something to stay on good terms with my mind. I would go after Felice.

I got up and put on my jacket. I patted my pocket to be sure I had my wallet. I walked down the hall. I looked at Mom standing in the kitchen, the greasehood over the stove casting light back on her cheeks. Her eyes were streaming. She'd been cutting onions. She smiled at me as I walked by and motioned me toward her, but she didn't speak. I knew why. She'd taught me that onion tears get worse if you open your mouth. It lets the fumes in. It's best to finish the peeling and chopping as quickly and silently as you can, or stop, if you must, to wash your hands and the knife, but you must not touch your eyes and you must not talk.

I didn't stop or walk into the steaming kitchen where I could hear the hamburger meat spitting and popping in the pan. "I'm late," I told her, and walked out the front door. She followed me to the doorway, still holding half an onion, but she never said a word.

Since I couldn't drive the car, I'd have to take a bus downtown to the Greyhound station. I would have to walk up to the mall where the city buses stopped. I stopped at a bank machine on the way and got out all it would give me of my summer savings. I had to walk past the Jim Dandy Fried Chicken place where Jeff had a part-time job. The walls of the little building were big plate-glass windows, with a huge, grinning, orange rooster painted on each one. I could see Jeff standing at the counter in his orange uniform, tossing two wings and a breast into a box for a woman in a white dress. I knew his skin was breaking out from spending so much time in the greasy air drinking free Coke from the machine, but from where I stood he looked perfect, like a commercial, the warming lights on the chicken and fries casting a glow on him from behind, like an electric halo. He patted the box of chicken and said something that looked like, "You bet," as the customer handed him her cash.

I wanted to go in and exchange a couple of words with him, but I knew we'd have to wisecrack, and I couldn't do that. So I rapped on the window with a quarter. He looked up, and I waved at him through the legs of the painted rooster. He gave me a nod and a stern look, in the don't-do-anything-to-besmirch-the-family-name manner he'd taken with me lately. I nodded back and walked on.

I didn't want to run into my father on his way home from work, and he got off at 6:25, so I had to catch the 6:10. I cut through Sears and Wyatt's Cafeteria, hurrying out the back of the mall. I walked across the big parking lot. It stretched like the desert at the base of Mt. Estrella, long and flat and black with white lines. There were clumps of cars, but they didn't begin to fill the vastness. A cool September wind was blowing across it, and the sky began to drizzle, but by the time I got to the bus, the sun was back, washed and lightened by the rain. The driver opened the door to let me sit inside while he finished his sandwich. All of the cars shone, and the raindrops on the windows of the bus sparked. I took this as a sign. Two women in high heels and skirts knocked on the door, and the driver let them in and said hi. They both had bags from Fashion Bar. I was looking at things sharply, and details kept coming into focus. First it had been Jeff in the window under the warming lights, then the shine of the wet cars and the bright colors on the shoppers' faces. A few more people trickled in before the driver put his newspaper down and started the bus. If I had been driving the Pinto, I could have been at the Greyhound station by now. We stopped at the corner of Weaver and Moody Boulevard, then got onto the highway, with no more stops until we were downtown.

Chapter
Sixteen

WHEN I GOT OFF AT THE STATION, THE WIND blew right through me. Cars were double-parked at the curb, and there was a big knot of people gathered near where the buses sat with their engines running, ready to depart. There was no line for tickets, though. The man behind the counter said I had a forty-five-minute wait, give or take, so I sat down at one of the chairs with tiny televisions on them. I put in a quarter for fifteen minutes' worth of "Gilligan's Island," but my attention kept wandering over the other people in the lobby.

There was a woman in a green plaid coat speaking in sign language to an older man, who was smoking and nodding. There was a hippie in a wheelchair at the candy machine, raising himself up to reach the coin slot. He looked pissed off.

I thought about it and decided that it made sense that a lot of people with disabilities would end up taking the bus, if they couldn't drive, or if they didn't have money for a car. The guy in the wheelchair had long hair in a ponytail, like Peg's, only his was blond. It made me restless to remember Peg and the way I had left her, so I got up before my quarter ran out and paced over to the crowd at the arrival/departure doors. There were delays being announced over the loudspeaker, and a lot of guys in uniform standing around. I had assumed that they were busdrivers, but now I saw that they were cops. The wheelchairs were thicker here than they were in the halls of the nursing home. Then I noticed the signs: WE WILL RIDE and EQUAL ACCESS. It was a demonstration. A woman with frizzy red hair and leg braces handed me a pink flyer that started:

Tired of buses with no lifts and narrow doors?
Tired of bus companies that will take our money
only if we travel with an able-bodied companion?
Tired of being treated like children?
FIGHT BACK!
NO BUSINESS AS USUAL...

As I scanned the words, I thought, "This sure sounds like Peg." I panicked—it sounded exactly like Peg. Even if she hadn't written it, she might be here. I knew I was being silly, but I turned and walked as fast as I decently could into the ladies room, to get out of sight of the demonstration.

There was Peg, sitting squarely in front of the only non-pay toilet stall, handing out flyers, wearing a fuzzy black sweater that I recognized as one of Ginny's. She was giving a flyer to a gray-haired woman in a pantsuit, talking slowly and patiently, as if she were determined to be understood. I could see the glint in her eye.

My first thought was that she was dangerous. My next was an impulse to go over and straighten up the messy pile of flyers in her lap. While I was still hesitating in the door, she saw me. I was scared. She looked more surprised. "Char," she said, "what are you doing here?"

I walked over to her, but I didn't bend to straighten the flyers. I realized that I knew better than to do that. I shifted my backpack to my other hand instead. "Going to get Felice."

I hadn't meant to phrase it that way. She looked at me quizzically, then I watched her remember how angry she was with me. She looked down at her lap. Someone had made her ponytail into a thick black braid. I wanted to hear what she had been going to say. My stomach was in knots. I touched her shoulder. "Peg, I'm sorry I walked out like that, without telling you or Ginny or anyone."

Peg snorted, handing me one of her bright pink flyers. "I should have expected it," she said.

The slow cut of her voice made my eyes tear up. I stared at the flyer and blinked until I could look at her. I tried again. "I just couldn't say anything." I was folding the flyer into smaller and smaller squares. "It was stupid. I miss you."

Peg shifted in her chair, looking over my shoulder at the doorway. A woman came in dragging a reluctant little boy by the hand. They both looked alarmed and slightly fascinated when they saw Peg, but she leaned way out to hand them a flyer. I had slipped mine into my back pocket. The woman took the little boy to the sink and started scrubbing his hands. Peg looked back at me. I couldn't read her face.

"I can't talk about this now," she said. "I'm busy." She unlocked her wheels.

I stepped out of her way, but I was still trying to talk. "Did you organize all this? How did you get here from the home?"

Peg was driving her chair with her back to me, so I had to concentrate to hear her. "Ginny finally got housing, so I moved in with her. No, I didn't organize the protest. There's a group. We've been writing letters ever since the food fight, and they helped us move." She bumped into the wall as she took the narrow turn to get out of the door and stopped for a moment. Behind me, the woman was saying over and over to her little boy, "Stop it, Walter. Shut up. Stop it. I told you to stop," and there were sharp little scuffling noises over the sound of running water.

Peg dug an old envelope out of the bag she kept wedged next to the arm of her chair. "Here," she said, "that's our address. You can come talk to me sometime." I moved to take the envelope from her, scared to open my mouth. Peg put the chair in gear again, "Maybe later you can bring Felice," she said as she headed toward the crowd.

I stuffed the envelope in my pocket, which was bulging with paper now. My fingers brushed the stiff edge of my ticket. My heart was pounding. I couldn't sort out the dizzy mix of shame and relief and anxiety, but I felt like I was breathing hot ash, so I pushed my way through the chanting crowd out one of the doors to the bus ports. I leaned against a concrete post and breathed the cold, exhaust-filled air. I had a bus to catch.

I scanned the row of buses, trying to spot mine. That was when I finally understood why not a single departure had been announced since I arrived. Every bus had a line of people behind it, sitting in wheelchairs or on blankets on the asphalt. Some of the buses were idling, causing the people behind them to be cloaked in black fumes, but neither buses nor protesters showed any sign of moving. Men in ties and suit coats the same silver as the buses were in a huddle with the police. I found the bus with "Albuquerque" on the front, but it was as hemmed in as the rest. I wasn't going anywhere for a while.

It was nearly dark when I saw Peg join a little clump behind a Chicago bus. I looked around for Ginny and saw her sitting on the sidewalk in front of Peg's bus, wearing a red corduroy jacket and singing into the wind. Every now and then a hoarse chant or a song would start in one of the lines behind the buses, or in the crowd in front of the doors, but not many voices picked it up. I had the feeling that they had been at this for hours. I couldn't believe that they would stay much longer.

I closed my eyes and huddled down against the post, trying to gather my patience and my sense of purpose. Instead, my mind's eye saw Felice getting on a bus, heading north. She is coming back to me, wearing her jeans and a new plum-colored sweater and tweed jacket for the fall. She looks perfect. She has a nylon bag packed with her summer things. She isn't carrying any rocks, except her big quartz key chain, but she has a folder full of geology notes and letters from me.

She has stayed up late the night before, drinking and saying goodbye to Tony, so she takes a window seat and drowses through the ride. The bus stops for gas at the truck stop where Louise works the cash register. Felice doesn't get anything to eat, but she does go in to use the bathroom. She buys a jack-a-lope postcard to send to Kenny. She gets back on the bus. I bring her down the highway and over the pass quickly, fluidly, the dreaming and the traveling blending into one feeling. I pull her bus into the very station where I am leaning on a post, waiting. The crowd parts like water for this one bus. It stops, people get off, but I couldn't wish that for her.

Felice sits in her seat, not anxious, not breathing, as still as I've ever seen her, waiting for me to decide. It was my vision, but I couldn't pull her off the bus simply because of the force of my need to see her, strong as it was, because that meant pulling her to Moody, to the locker next to Beverly's, her mother's fires, and Mr. Coolig in geology class cracking his peanuts. Even in my dream Felice fought coming back to all that.

I was about done with dreaming Felice. I knew her for real. We couldn't go back to sneaking into bars so she could dance with the guys while I watched. We'd even passed the slow, sweet point of dancing together in the living room. We'd passed out of our child lives, but there wasn't anyplace else for us to go, not yet. I was furious at her for leaving me stranded in Moody, but I didn't have any other real bright ideas. This thing with Tony was a slap in the face, though. She probably thought it was necessary.

She is still sitting there motionless on the frozen bus. I was still leaning on cold concrete. Then, I let her go. I sent her on. New folks board, and the bus pulls out, but it doesn't keep heading north, and it doesn't turn around. It takes an exit I'd never noticed before and drives on a two-lane highway all the way to someplace where there are houses made of pumice and Felice's new tweed jacket will keep her as warm as she needs to be all winter long. The town is half-circled by volcanoes, and each of its beaches has the distinct color of a different rock ground by the sea.

THAT LEFT ME at the station. The bullhorns snapped me back into the immediate world. The silver-coated bus men had disappeared, but the cops had massed up and were moving in. The chanting had gotten louder, and the folks behind the buses moved closer to each other. The ones that could linked arms. There was a little flurry of people trying to snatch blankets and call out to friends, then protesters were being grabbed and shoved into the back of a police van. It had a ramp on it, all set up for wheelchairs, but the cops went for people who were able-bodied first. Somebody—I didn't know if it was a driver or a protester—climbed into one of the buses and started honking the horn. I saw the frizzy red-haired woman who had first handed me a flyer go limp with a cop's arms under her shoulders. He dragged her into the van with her leg braces bouncing on the ramp. I was shocked—I'd never seen anybody arrested before. I looked for Peg. She was in the middle of a huddle of cops.

Ginny was yelling from the front of the legal crowd on the sidewalk. "Peg! Don't get yourself beat up! Show them where the damn switch is."

Peg called back something that didn't carry over the honking, but she might have been reminding Ginny to water the plants. Ginny nodded, then started to cry.

Two cops were on their knees by the wheels of Peg's chair, trying to figure out how to make the thing move, and two were pushing and yanking on the handles. For a moment I could see Peg's face; she looked like she was cussing them out. Finally somebody found the right combination of switches, and the chair lurched forward over the hand of one of the cops on the ground, who gave out a screech.

The van was almost full by the time they got Peg up the ramp, and they slammed the door shut after her. The van pulled out, and another one backed in to take its place. Behind me in the station, a departure was being announced on the loudspeaker. Protesters were chanting about the people united, and I found myself yelling at the top of my lungs. I looked over at Ginny—she was yelling, too, and holding hands with the tall hippie from the candy machine. The woman behind her was stroking her hair. The arrests had slowed down, and the cops were making a line in front of the sidewalk crowd. A few passengers straggled out from the station to get on one of the buses. It pulled out. We booed and surged forward, but the cops held the line, and the bus was gone.

I was still standing behind my post, howling. Some of the protesters gave me nervous glances. I must have sounded out of control. The honking had stopped, and a tall young cop with a bullhorn was telling us to disperse. I picked up my backpack and ran away from the crowd, too stirred up to stand still anymore. I kicked over an ashtray on my way through the lobby, slammed out the glass door, and ran down one of the empty streets between the buildings. The wind was still high. I had a hard time breathing as I ran, so I concentrated on pulling the air in and letting it out. I could feel fury moving me, keeping me running, until it started to leave me with my breath. I came to the big park across from the statehouse, and sat down on one of the benches, gasping and wheezing. There were pigeons in front of me pecking the worn grass. My mind was groping, trying to figure out what I should do next. I started to feel embarrassed, as if I had borrowed somebody else's anger because I couldn't come up with any of my own. I hadn't even checked with Ginny to see if she needed anything. Still, something had changed in me.

The pigeons were giving out little moans and cries. I found that annoying, so I got up and started walking down the street. The haze in my head gathered and cleared, then gathered again as I walked. Finally a Moody bus came by, and I got on. I had to reach past the stiff Greyhound ticket to find change for the fare.

When the bus got off the highway, it drove down Moody Boulevard. All around me were the lighted houses of my neighborhood. I got off at the mall and walked down the hill toward home. The shift had changed at Jim Dandy, so I didn't see Jeff as I passed.

I told Mom I had been on a long walk. She said there was some supper left. I wasn't hungry, though. I went into my room and took the screen off the window so the wind could blow in. I put on my nightgown. I pulled back the sheets on my bed. I found the grocery bag full of Felice's rocks and dumped them onto the mattress. I got in with them and pulled the blankets up to my chin. I felt around until I found the little wedge of chalcedony and slipped it under my nightgown. It was cold at first, but slowly warmed on my skin. I slept with it tucked under one breast. My dreams were sharp.

Photo by Susan Wilson

Susan Stinson grew up in Colorado. Her fiction and poetry have appeared in several anthologies and magazines, including *Sinister Wisdom* and *The Kenyon Review*. She is also the author of *Belly Songs: In Celebration of Fat Women* and *Martha Moody*, a novel to be published by Spinsters Ink in 1995. She lives near Northampton, MA.